"Please, Brooks," Melissa begged.

"I just want to talk to you."

"I thought you didn't have time to talk," Brooks said. "Shouldn't you be at practice right now? Or memorizing chemistry tables or something?"

"This is where I want to be," Melissa said. "With you."

"I doubt that," Brooks said. He stared down at the floor.

"I'm sorry," Melissa continued after a long silence. "Couldn't I come in for just a minute and talk to you?"

"Where were you when I wanted to talk?" Brooks mumbled.

"I know I wasn't there before," Melissa said. "But I am now."

"Mel." Brooks sighed. "I'm not going to set myself up to be hurt again."

"Please!" Melissa begged, but the door closed firmly and she heard the lock click.

Don't miss these books
in the exciting FRESHMAN DORM series

Freshman Dorm
Freshman Lies
Freshman Guys
Freshman Nights
Freshman Dreams
Freshman Games

And, coming soon . . .

Freshman Secrets

FRESHMAN LOVES

LINDA A. COONEY

HarperPaperbacks
A Division of HarperCollins*Publishers*

This is a work of fiction. The characters, incidents, and dialogues are products of the author's imagination and are not to be construed as real. Any resemblance to actual events or persons, living or dead, is entirely coincidental.

HarperPaperbacks *A Division of* HarperCollins*Publishers*
10 East 53rd Street, New York, N.Y. 10022

Cover art by Tony Greco

First printing: March 1991

Printed in the United States of America

HarperPaperbacks and colophon are trademarks of HarperCollins*Publishers*

10 9 8 7 6 5 4 3 2

One

....

"*First call! Women's four by one hundred meters!*" a voice blared over the University of Springfield stadium loudspeaker.

Melissa McDormand felt a surge of raw energy shoot through her body. Her heart started pumping wildly. After months of training, self-denial, and aching muscles, she was finally going to be put to the test.

Melissa still had several minutes before her race, the eight hundred meters, but she had to begin her warmup right away. She wanted to find a quiet place, but that would be impossible in the crowd. There seemed to be as many people roaming around the track as there were up in the stands. University of Springfield runners, dressed like Melissa in purple and gold warmups, jogged nervously up and down the eight-lane track, trying to ignore the red-suited athletes from Western U who were doing the same thing. In green and white, runners from State huddled around their coach for a last-minute pep talk.

A glint of gold over by the fence caught Melissa's eye. Standing on tiptoe to see over the crowd, Melissa saw it was the reflection of sunlight on blond curls. Melissa knew those curls—so soft, yet surrounding a ruggedly masculine face, the face of her boyfriend, Brooks Baldwin.

Melissa pushed through the crowd to get closer. She saw Brooks lounging against the fence, his solid, well-defined muscles pushing against the fabric of his flannel shirt and faded jeans. As usual, he wore muddy hiking boots. Before Melissa could raise her hand to wave, Brooks caught her eye and smiled.

"Last call! Women's four by one hundred meters!" blared the loudspeaker. The jumble of red, purple, gold, green, and white began to organize itself as most runners cleared the track and others unzipped their warmup jackets, heading for the staggered starting lines.

Melissa's coach, Terrence Meeham, stood inside the oval, near the starting line, holding his clipboard. "Runners, take your marks," Terry called. The race official pointed his starter's pistol in the air and fired. Eight women tore down the first straightaway, arms and legs churning.

Ignoring them, Melissa closed her eyes and began to breathe deeply, rhythmically. *Inhale, two, three, four. Exhale, two, three, four.* Over and over she repeated the breathing exercise until her muscles relaxed and her mind let go. Then she began to screen out the rest of the world—the track, the officials, the excited crowd, and the other runners.

Getting rid of her doubts was much harder. Though Melissa had run a powerhouse four hundred meters in high school, this was the first time she'd be running the eight hundred meters. Most of her teammates considered this the hardest race of all because it was right in the middle distancewise. A runner had to have the endurance of a long-distance runner and the speed of a sprinter to go those two laps around the track, about a half-mile.

Inhale, two, three, four. Exhale, two, three, four. Melissa knew she could do it. Terry had drilled the team for months, pushing them through day after day of grueling workouts until they were exhausted. By comparison, running a single race should seem easy. But for Melissa, there was so much at stake that it could never seem easy. Melissa was pre-med *and* on a track scholarship. That put her in a double bind. If she didn't keep up her grades, she'd get kicked off the team, and if she didn't do well in track, she'd get kicked out of school. She had to stay disciplined all the time or everything she'd worked so hard for would vanish.

But for once she wasn't worried. Melissa had never felt so relaxed before a race, so able to shut out doubts and distractions. And she knew why. It was because Brooks was nearby, supporting her, and cheering her on.

It was hard to believe she'd given Brooks such a hard time in the beginning. He'd practically had to use a sledgehammer to crack open her hard shell. It wasn't that she hadn't been interested or attracted; she'd just been scared. Scared of getting involved for the first time, scared of letting down her guard, and, most of all, scared of letting anything or anyone distract her from her goals. Melissa still felt that way sometimes, but certainly not right then.

Inhale, two, three, four. Exhale, two, three, four. Melissa opened her eyes feeling calm and sure of herself. She was ready.

"Yo, Melissa!" screamed a voice from far away.

Squinting in the bright sunlight, Melissa scanned

the stadium to see where the voice was coming from.

"Melissa!" screamed several voices together. Melissa finally spotted the source of the sound. Up in the bleachers, waving madly, were Melissa's roommate, Winnie Gottlieb, and Winnie's two best friends, Faith Crowley and KC Angeletti.

Even from a distance, Winnie's outfit was hard to miss. Her spiky dark hair was tucked under a long purple-and-gold U of S stocking cap. She wore a bright purple sweatshirt and gold Lycra tights and waved a purple-and-gold U of S banner. She looked like a sports-crazed elf.

"You can do it!" Winnie screamed through cupped hands.

Melissa's usually serious face broke into a broad grin. She hadn't allowed herself to get close to many people, but she couldn't help liking her crazy, sloppy, brilliant roommate.

Melissa dropped forward so she could stretch out her hamstrings before the race. She'd pulled a hamstring in practice in the fall, so she had to be especially careful. Then she spread her legs wide and bent over to stretch her spine. From that position, she had a great view of Brooks. He looked just as good upside down as he did right side up.

A pair of purple legs stepped in front of Melissa,

blocking her view of Brooks. "Who's the hunk?" asked a voice from above.

Melissa rose and turned around. Her teammate, Caitlin Bruneau, stood before her, her frizzy brown hair pulled back in a ponytail. A junior, Caitlin was the lead middle-distance runner and had taken a special liking to Melissa. Melissa was flattered that an upperclassman, and a track star, should pay her so much attention.

"That's my boyfriend," she said softly.

"Not bad!" Caitlin teased. "Not bad at all! Though I'm surprised you have the time."

"Well, actually I don't," Melissa admitted, "but somehow I seem to find it."

"That's always the way it starts," Caitlin said.

"The way what starts?" asked Melissa.

Caitlin shook her head in mock seriousness. "First a few stolen moments here, some candlelit dinners there, and suddenly you start dreaming of him instead of crossing the finish line."

"Oh, that would never happen to me," Melissa said seriously. "When I run, I run. I don't think of anything else."

"Not even those cherubic curls?" Caitlin asked.

"Stop! He'll hear you!" Melissa said, laughing in embarrassment. "And anyway, you know me better than that. I am not a woman. I am a *running machine!"*

"That's the spirit!" Caitlin said.

"We're gonna do it!" Melissa shouted.

Caitlin whooped and pumped her fist.

"First call, women's eight hundred meters!" blared the loudspeaker.

"That's us," Caitlin said, unzipping her jacket. "Good luck."

"I'll be right on your tail," Melissa said.

"Try and catch me," Caitlin said, jogging away.

Melissa followed Caitlin to find Terry. He stood with three electronic stopwatches hanging around his neck.

"Lane four, McDormand," Terry said as Melissa approached.

Melissa nodded.

"You've been looking good out there," Terry said. "Just run it like you did in practice. Use your kick. Good luck."

"Thanks, Coach," Melissa said, trotting away. She peeled off her warmups and dropped them by the side of the track. Then she found her mark and began to hop up and down, shaking her shoulders to stay loose.

"Last call, women's eight hundred meters!" came the announcement.

Melissa tightened her ponytail and adjusted her sweatband. Out of the corner of her eye, she could see Caitlin warming up, but Melissa ignored her and all the other runners. All Melissa saw were the white lines stretching out ahead of her. Then she allowed herself one last look at Brooks. He was gazing at her intently, one hand above his eyes to block the glare. When he saw Melissa turn, he gave her a huge smile.

Melissa felt as if she could run to the moon if she had to. She couldn't wait for the gun to go off.

"Runners, take your marks!" called Terry from the center of the oval.

Melissa placed her left foot forward and took a deep breath.

BANG! The gunshot crackled through the air and Melissa was flying down the straightaway. She felt loose, light, flowing. As she rounded the corner she saw a purple streak in front of her move to the inside lane. It was Caitlin, dominating the race as usual, but Melissa didn't worry about her. Melissa just kept up her rhythm, making sure Caitlin didn't pull too far ahead. Vaguely, Melissa was aware of other runners close behind her, but she didn't worry about them, either. She just kept seeing the finish line in her mind, her chest breaking through the white tape, and Brooks's smile.

A bell rang, signaling the second lap. Melissa's breathing was still calm and regular. She didn't feel winded at all. Caitlin was still ahead, but only a few meters, and the pack behind her had thinned out and spread along the track.

They turned onto the back stretch. Melissa's legs were pumping like pistons, strong and regular, as she waited to make her move.

As soon as they'd rounded the final corner, Melissa went into overdrive. Her legs exploded in a blur of motion as she came up on Caitlin's right shoulder. Caitlin, aware of Melissa trying to pass her, picked up speed.

Melissa was just half a pace behind at that point, but the white tape was racing toward them so fast that she didn't have time to overtake Caitlin. Caitlin crossed the finish line with Melissa right on her heels.

The crowd cheered as the two runners continued around the oval, slowing their pace. Breathing heavily, her heart still pounding, Melissa slapped Caitlin on the back.

Caitlin gave her a wry grin. "Not bad for a freshman!" she said.

Melissa smiled back. "I wonder how we did."

"I'd say about one minute fifty-two seconds, or

thereabouts," Caitlin said. "Wait, here's Terry with his stopwatch collection. He'll tell us."

Terry approached the girls, grinning broadly. "Now I've got two stars!" he said. "This is going to be a very good season. I can feel it already."

"How'd we do?" Caitlin asked.

"One minute fifty-one point five five seconds," Terry told her, holding up one stopwatch. Then he held up the other to Melissa. "One fifty-one point nine three."

Melissa screamed and jumped up and down in excitement. "That's the best I've ever done!" she cried. "I can't believe it! I just can't believe it!"

"Believe it," said Terry. "You were less than half a second behind Caitlin." He turned to the older girl. "You'd better watch your back," he warned, still grinning.

"I've got eyes all over my head," Caitlin tossed back confidently. "Well, I'd better get ready for the four by four-hundred-meter relay. See ya later."

"First call, men's eight hundred meters," announced the voice.

"See you at practice tomorrow," Terry said, heading back for the center of the oval. "It's going to be heavy duty, so get some sleep."

Melissa nodded and grinned. "Brooks!" she

called, running back toward the crowd. "Brooks!" She couldn't find him. "Brooks!"

A pair of strong arms grabbed her by the waist and spun her around and around. Melissa recognized the delicious, familiar scent of Brooks's aftershave and breathed it in deeply.

"Looking for me?" he asked as he gently lowered her to the ground.

"I'm all sweaty," Melissa started to apologize, but Brooks just pulled her closer and pressed his lips against hers. His kiss was so soft, so delicate that Melissa melted against him, forgetting to be embarrassed that her track suit was soaking wet.

Up in the bleachers, Winnie screamed at the top of her lungs. *"Aaaaaaaah!"* she shrieked, waving her banner. *"All right, Melissa!"* She climbed up on her seat and started jumping up and down.

"Sit down, Winnie!" said KC sharply. "You're shaking the bench!"

Ignoring KC, Winnie jumped up and down even harder and continued to scream.

"If this bench breaks . . ." KC warned.

"What?" Winnie challenged her. "What are you going to do, sue me?"

"Maybe," KC shot back.

"See you in court!" Winnie sang, sticking out

her tongue. *"Aaaaaaaaah!"* she screamed again. *"Aaaaaaaah!"*

Faith had a feeling Winnie was no longer screaming for Melissa.

"I wish she'd stop that," said KC in annoyance to Faith. "What's she doing, primal-scream therapy?"

"Winnie's just excited," Faith said, though she was equally concerned about her friend's behavior.

"Well, it's totally undignified," KC said. "Not that that's ever stopped her before."

"Don't be so hard on her," Faith pleaded. "She's been freaking out ever since she broke up with Josh. She's really beside herself."

"And whose fault is that?" KC asked tartly. "She could have had him if she'd wanted to. But no, she'd rather two-time Josh *and* Travis and see how long she could get away with it."

"Which was not very long, thanks to you," said Winnie from up on the bench. Faith wasn't sure when Winnie had stopped screaming and started listening.

"Don't blame me for your dishonesty," KC said.

"You know, I'm *glad* I threw you in the pool at Winter Formal," Winnie snapped. "Too bad that sorority snob Marielle Danner fished you out again."

Faith nervously tucked a strand of silky blond hair

back into her French braid. Things weren't going the way she had planned at all. She had arranged to have her two best friends come to watch Melissa's race, hoping it would bring them back together. But it was all Faith could do to keep them from tearing each other apart.

As if that weren't bad enough, at that very moment her ex-boyfriend, Brooks, was kissing his new girlfriend, Melissa, right in front of Faith's eyes. She tried to convince herself that it really didn't matter. Faith had been the one to break it off with her high-school boyfriend, so she had no right to feel bad that he'd moved on to someone else. She didn't have time for a relationship just then, anyway. The theater-arts department was giving her all the work she could handle, in class and out.

"Please!" Faith begged her friends, willing her attention away from Melissa and Brooks. "Can't we try to forget about what happened last semester and just start over?"

"Hmph," Winnie replied, hopping off the bench and sitting down with a thump.

KC just crossed her arms over her chest and pretended to be absorbed in the next race.

"Oh, great!" Faith sighed. She turned back to Winnie. "So, any word from Travis?"

Winnie shook her head. "Gone without a trace,"

she said. "I went to find him at the rooming house, but his landlady said he'd packed up and left the very next day. I'm pretty sure he went to L.A."

Though Winnie was smiling, her eyes glittered with a strange light. She started poking her gold Lycraed leg with the wooden stick of her banner. "You know he wrote a song about me? Maybe I'll hear it on the radio someday. Or maybe it will reach number one on the charts and they'll interview Travis about it on a talk show and he'll say it was about me, and then *I'll* be famous, so don't worry about me. I know you're worried about me."

"I'm not worried about you," Faith lied. "You're going to be all right. You just need a little time to recover. Anyway, I know Josh was the one you really cared about."

"Well, that's true," Winnie admitted, "but I can handle it. I mean, I *could* handle it if I didn't have to see him every day in the dorm."

"How's he been?" Faith asked.

"Oh, you know, very friendly but cool. The fire has definitely gone out."

"And you were the one with the hose," KC jibed from the other side of Faith.

"I doused *you* pretty good," Winnie shot back. "It was the funniest thing I've ever seen!"

"There was nothing funny about it," KC said,

bristling. "You nearly ruined my chances of being voted freshman princess at Winter Formal."

Faith covered her ears, feeling helpless to stop her friends' bickering.

"Thank goodness I have some *real* friends who help me out of a crisis instead of getting me into one," KC continued. "If it hadn't been for Marielle, I would have lost the election *and* my chances of getting into the Tri Betas."

"Oh, yes, your real, *true* friend, Marielle," Winnie said sarcastically. "She really strikes me as the sincere type. You sure know how to choose your friends."

"I also know how to unchoose them," KC said stiffly.

"Where are you going?" Winnie taunted. "To talk to your boyfriend, Peter Dvorsky?" Winnie held her hands to her mouth in mock embarrassment. "Oops! I forgot. He's not your boyfriend. You dumped him to go to Winter Formal with that mannequin, Warren Manning."

Taking a deep breath, KC stared Winnie down and said in a low, angry voice, "At least *I* can still get a date. Goodbye, Faith," she said pointedly, and stomped down the broad steps of the bleachers.

"Hey, look, Faith!" Winnie shouted, seemingly oblivious to KC's departure. "I'm a hurdler!" She stood up and leaped over her seat, colliding with the people sitting behind them. "Maybe I should go out for track next season," Winnie said cheerfully, ignoring the dirty looks she was getting from the people she'd bumped into.

Faith fought back tears of frustration. Her friends might be willing to throw away their friendship, but she wasn't. There *had* to be something she could do, some way to make them realize what they were losing. Too bad she had no idea what that something was.

Two

·····················

"**I** think there are more letters addressed to us than to Dear 'Abbey,' " Lauren Turnbell-Smythe said to Dash Ramirez as she hauled another sack of letters across the dingy, crowded office of the *U of S Weekly Journal*.

Dash laughed. Lauren's wispy light brown hair fell over her face as she leaned down to pick up the sack, but Dash placed a strong, gentle hand on her arm.

"I'll get that," he offered. "You'll hurt your back."

Lauren's violet eyes peered at Dash through wire-rimmed glasses. As usual, his face was shadowed by

several days' growth of beard. With the red bandanna tied over his forehead and his long dark hair
pulled back into a ponytail he reminded Lauren of a
sexy pirate.

"I thought we were equals," she teased. "Part-
ners. Are you saying I'm not strong enough to lift
this?"

"Oh, excuse me," Dash said, making a courtly
bow.

Lauren lifted the sack and threw it to Dash.

He caught the sack and pretended to fall.

"Vive la différence," said Dash.

Lauren gazed up at Dash in his baggy green army
pants and distressed leather jacket. A streetwise
sophomore, Dash had always made fun of her for
coming from a wealthy family and joining a sorority. She'd always felt she had to bend over backward
to prove she wasn't a superficial snob. With so little
in common, the last thing she'd expected was that
they'd fall in love.

Lauren leaned over Dash's cluttered desk. An
empty Styrofoam cup ringed with coffee stains clat-
tered hollowly to the floor, followed by several
dozen sheets of paper, half a stale donut, and some
ancient cigarette butts. "I like what you've done
with the place," Lauren said, grinning. "Who's your
decorator?"

Dash grinned back as he replaced the papers on his desk and threw the rest away. "I don't know anything about decorators, unlike some people I know."

"I certainly don't know anything about them anymore," Lauren argued. "I'm just a lowly chambermaid."

Lauren's mother had cut her off without a cent when Lauren got herself kicked out of the exclusive Tri Beta sorority. Now Lauren had to earn pocket money by working as a maid at the Springfield Mountain Inn.

"Don't worry, Cinderella," Dash said, sweeping her into his arms. "Kiss me before midnight and you'll turn into a princess."

Though Lauren was aware of the amused stares of several *Weekly Journal* staffers, she leaned backward in Dash's arms, delighting in her feeling of security. Dash would never let her fall. He leaned forward and kissed her hard on the lips. Lauren felt her mind go blank except for little firecracker flashes of light going off in her head.

The sound of applause brought her back to earth. Lauren opened her eyes and saw Dash's face just a few inches from hers. "You look like a princess to me," he said softly. Then she saw that everyone in the newsroom was giving them a standing ovation.

Lauren smiled. "I guess the show is over," she said amid the laughter of the amused staffers.

Dash gently lifted her back to an upright position. "Let's take a look at these letters," he said.

As everyone else turned back to work, Lauren and Dash started ripping open envelopes.

"I can't believe the response we've gotten to our hazing article," said Lauren as she quickly scanned each letter. "Listen to this one." She read aloud. " 'I was enraged to hear that hazing is alive and well on the U of S campus. I thought torture went out with the Dark Ages, but maybe Omega Delta Tau is still living in the Dark Ages. Hopefully this incident will strike a death knell for fraternities everywhere.' "

"Here's another one," said Dash. He read: " 'It's bad enough that our society idolizes those blessed with good bone structure, good skin, and good hair. But is being too fat, too thin, too short, or too tall punishable by death? The recent hazing of Howard Benmann proves, unfortunately, that this is the case, at least at ODT. It's time those frat brothers realized they don't make the rules. I hope the guilty parties are punished to the full extent of the law.' "

"This is great," Lauren said, pausing over the huge pile of letters. "It's so satisfying knowing that our article has really made a difference."

"It wasn't just the article," Dash said. "It was your quick thinking. If you hadn't caused a commotion when the frat boys were locking Howard in the trunk, he might have been in there a long time. He could have suffocated!"

Lauren thought back to the night the previous semester when she'd waited in the bushes outside the ODT fraternity house. On a tip from KC, she'd learned that ODT was planning to haze skinny, awkward Howard Benmann to make sure he didn't join their fraternity. After getting him dangerously drunk, they stripped him down to his underwear and locked him in the trunk of Mark Geisslinger's Volvo. Lauren, who'd been watching nearby, did the only thing she could think of. She'd screamed bloody murder, frightening the ODT brothers away. Howard, shivering, sick, and nearly naked, had been rescued from the trunk a few minutes later.

It had been tremendously satisfying to put Mark and the others in their place. As a result of the article, the culprits had been forced to make public apologies. They'd also been fined and were each required to perform twenty hours of community service.

"It was all in a day's work," said Lauren modestly.

"But tomorrow's another day," Dash said. "What

is the famous journalistic team of Ramirez and Turnbell-Smythe going to do for a follow-up?"

"You mean Turnbell-Smythe and Ramirez," Lauren corrected him.

"I'm just trying to get ahead," Dash said, an innocent look on his face. "When you come from my neighborhood, you have to work that much harder. Some of us weren't born with all the advantages."

"I'll take advantage of *you,*" Lauren said, leaning forward to tickle him. She pushed aside the soft leather of his jacket and wiggled her fingers over his flat stomach. Even through his ink-stained T-shirt, she could feel how firm his abdominal muscles were. As Lauren tickled Dash, he doubled over, laughing hysterically.

"Hey! Hey!" Dash said, holding up his arms. "I surrender! You win! Turnbell-Smythe and Ramirez sounds good to me!"

"Okay," said Lauren, perching on the edge of his desk, "let's get down to business. I don't want to do any fluff. We're off to a good start with the Bickford Lane and the hazing articles. I'd like to do something like that again. You know, socially conscious." Before she'd finished speaking, Lauren blushed. She'd never been able to take charge before, yet there she was, telling the assistant editor of the *U of S Weekly Journal* what to do. And to think that just a few short months earlier she hadn't even been sure if she was good enough to write for the paper!

"I was thinking along the same lines," Dash said. "You know, with the new openness in the Soviet-bloc countries, there have been a lot of Russian and East European exchange students coming here. Maybe we could do a feature on them. For example, is capitalism living up to all their expectations?"

"That's not bad," Lauren said. "I'd better start writing this stuff down." She felt around Dash's desk for a pad and a pen but instead turned up another Styrofoam cup, this one crushed and still leaking coffee. "Give me a break, Ramirez!" she said, tossing the cup in the trash can. "It's bad enough you never clean your desk, but I can't believe you're still drinking out of Styrofoam cups! Don't you know that when they disintegrate they release chemicals into the air that destroy the ozone layer?"

"I know, I know," Dash said wearily. "I don't buy them anymore. Those are old ones. I only use paper now. Hey, that gives me an idea. I saw something on the news the other night about plastics. A lot of manufacturers now claim on their packaging that their plastic products are biodegradable, but it turns out that some of those claims are misleading."

"Maybe plastics manufacturers are getting nervous that people will start buying paper products instead because paper can be recycled," Lauren said.

"That's my theory," Dash said.

"But do you really think the plastics manufacturers are deliberately lying to make sure they don't lose business?"

"It sounds like a question that needs to be answered!" Dash exclaimed. "And I think we're just the people to do it."

"There's a recycling center on campus," Lauren said. "Maybe we can ask someone there whether these plastics really are biodegradable."

"I believe we have an article," Dash said. "What do you say we make a date to go over to the recycling center? Or we could just make a date."

Dash pushed aside a pile of papers and sat beside Lauren on his desk. Then he pulled her close.

"You can recycle my plastics anytime," she said seductively, kissing his ear.

Dash started to kiss her neck, then suddenly jumped to his feet. "What time is it?" he asked.

Lauren looked at her watch. "Almost three-thirty."

Dash slapped the side of his head. "The editors' meeting started ten minutes ago, and I'm supposed to be there! What was I thinking of?"

Lauren smiled knowingly.

"Oh yes," Dash said, returning the smile. "I'm sure our editor-in-chief will understand completely." He bit her lightly on the earlobe. "Later."

Lauren turned back to Dash's messy desk and started to look for her backpack. She was sure she'd put it down when she came in, but it was nowhere to be found. It was probably hidden under a pile of papers or a moldy Twinkie. Lauren skimmed through the papers, trying to organize them into neat piles at the same time.

Her eye was caught by a paper smaller than the rest—pink, scented, with words written on it in Spanish. What was it? Did Dash have another girlfriend? Lauren didn't want to believe it, couldn't believe it, but she scanned the foreign words anyway, looking for a clue.

Lauren laughed at herself when she saw the signature. *Mama.* She didn't need to major in Spanish to know that one. At least she couldn't be accused of reading it, she rationalized, since she didn't understand it. There were, however, several words she recognized. The date—last Monday—was in English. *Moreno's*—that was a local restaurant. And *7:30 p.m. Sabado.* Even Lauren knew that meant Saturday. She ran her eyes over the page once more and saw two other words that made sense: *Papa* and *Anna.* Lauren knew Dash had a sister named Anna.

Come to think of it, that was the only fact she knew about his family.

As the letter's meaning became clear, Lauren found herself feeling more and more confused. Dash's family was coming to visit and he hadn't said a word about it, let alone invited her to join them at Moreno's. Not that she should expect him to. He never talked about his family, and she'd never asked. So why did she feel betrayed?

Three

．．．．．．．．．．．．．．．．．．．．．．．．

*C*runch! *Crunch! Crunch!* went the gravel beneath KC's patent-leather flats as she walked across the parking lot of the Beanery, Springfield's local coffeehouse. She checked her watch, as she had every two minutes since she'd left the stadium. She didn't want to be late for her date with Marielle. Marielle, a Tri Beta sister, had behaved snobbishly to KC in the past, but recently she had proven herself to be a true friend.

Like Winnie used to be, KC thought.

"Used to" is right. What kind of friend destroys all

your chances of being voted freshman princess when she knows that's more important to you than anything?

An angry friend. A friend who felt betrayed when you told Josh her secret. A friend who was always ready to cheer you up when you were depressed, even if it involved climbing through your bedroom window in the middle of the night to sing you a silly song she'd made up herself. A friend who lent you seventy dollars in high school and never asked for the money back.

She probably just forgot she lent it to me, KC considered. *Winnie's like that.*

Maybe she didn't forget. Maybe she'd rather make you happy than spend the money herself.

But that was all over now, KC reminded herself, and Winnie was the one who'd ended it. KC had impressed all the judges at Winter Formal, including Courtney Conner, president of the Tri Betas, and was a shoo-in for freshman princess. But Winnie had pushed her into the Springfield Mountain Inn's swimming pool, ruining her dress and makeup. KC thought she'd lost all hope of winning, but Marielle had helped her turn defeat into victory. Marielle had lent KC her dress, redone her makeup, and restyled her hair. KC was able to return to the formal looking even more gorgeous than ever and had won the crown. Since then KC and Marielle had been inseparable.

Just like you and Winnie used to be, the voice reminded her again. *And now when she needs you more than ever, when she's teetering on the brink, you're just going to let her fall.*

KC felt a lump rise in her throat. Why was she still thinking about Winnie? Winnie obviously didn't care about her anymore, so KC wasn't going to waste any more time getting sappy about some stupid stuff that had happened in high school. It was time to move on to a new friend who cared about her *now.*

KC's watch said 3:29. She was a minute early. KC pushed open the heavy wooden front door of the Beanery and breathed in the familiar aromas of rich coffee, chocolate, and cinnamon.

She headed for the main dining room and scanned the tables. Marielle was already seated near the empty stage at a small round table. Her bright red fingernails perfectly matched her chic red suit. Her straight brown hair hung sleekly over one eye, and her charm bracelet jangled as she raised a cup of espresso to her lips.

KC waved and Marielle's face lit up.

"I hope you don't mind that I ordered without you," Marielle said in her twangy voice as KC took her seat, "but I needed caffeine like you wouldn't believe. I pulled an all-nighter last night trying to get a paper in for English."

"I know what that's like," KC agreed. "Except for my business courses, everything I'm taking is such a grind. I mean, how many papers can one person write?"

Marielle lifted a plastic-coated menu from between the ketchup and the napkin dispenser and handed it to KC. "Here," she said, "order anything you want. It's on me."

"Don't be silly," KC said. "If anything, I should take *you* out, after all you've done for me."

Please, please, please, she thought, *don't take me up on my offer unless you're planning to spend less than a dollar and forty-seven cents.* She didn't know what she would do if Marielle agreed to let her pay.

Marielle waved a delicate hand dismissively. "I'm feeling very generous right now because Daddy sent me my allowance, and you'd be *too* rude if you refused me."

"Are you sure?" KC asked, hoping her relief didn't show in her face.

"Order!" Marielle commanded. "Price is no object."

At that moment, a waiter appeared with his pad.

KC ordered a piece of lemon meringue pie and a diet cola.

"I wish I could eat like that," Marielle sighed as the pie was placed in front of KC. The meringue alone stood three inches high, not counting several inches of lemon filling. "You're so lucky you can eat whatever you want and not gain weight."

KC sipped her soda and smiled. An awkward moment of silence filled the space between them.

"I like those earrings," KC finally said. "Are they new?"

"Oh, yes," said Marielle, looking embarrassed as she fingered the gold seashells clipped to her earlobes. "I splurged. I know my dad's going to kill me when he sees the bill. I guess I'll have to convince him it's an early birthday present."

KC tried to cover her jealousy at Marielle's rich and generous father. "They're lovely," she said warmly.

Marielle immediately removed the earrings and handed them to KC. "Try them on," she offered. "If you like, you can borrow them. I've got plenty more." Then she leaned in closer. "So tell me," she whispered, "what's the scoop on you and Warren Manning? You two looked so good together at Winter Formal—just like the cover of a magazine. Has he asked you out again?"

KC shook her head. "We really weren't right for

each other," she said simply. "There just wasn't any chemistry between us."

"How about between *us?*" asked a deep male voice above their heads.

KC looked up. Towering over them was a tall, well-built young man. His skin was deeply tanned and he had long, shaggy blond hair. He wore ripped jeans and a torn T-shirt that read Surfin' USA. Behind him was an olive-skinned young man, equally tall and muscular, with short, dark, curly hair and penetrating brown eyes.

"Do I know you?" KC asked the two.

"Not yet," said the blond, "but we know you. I'm Steve Powell, and this is my good buddy Eric Bitterman."

"We've got you up in our lockers," Eric said, grinning.

"Oh, are you on a team?" Marielle asked, looking up at them coyly through her thick dark eyelashes.

"We read about you in the *Weekly Journal,* too," Steve continued, ignoring Marielle. "So you're freshman princess?"

"Yes, she is," Marielle said, jumping into the conversation. "And if you want to schedule an interview, you'll have to go through me. I'm her publicity agent." Marielle giggled and looked up at the guys expectantly, waiting for some reaction.

"That was a joke," she explained after a short silence.

Steve and Eric looked at her blankly.

Marielle smiled sweetly. "Never mind," she said, tearing open a package of artificial sweetener and dumping it into her espresso. Then she stirred it noisily with her spoon.

"So, you're freshman princess?" Steve repeated to KC, as if Marielle had never spoken.

KC nodded shyly.

"You need a footman?" Eric piped up, kneeling beside her. "I give great foot massages. Nothing more relaxing right before a big exam."

"No, thank you," KC said, embarrassed.

"Don't mind him," Steve said as Eric got back on his feet. "He's just goofing around."

"You ought to come see us play sometime," Eric said. "There are only a few games left before the season ends."

"What team?" KC asked.

The guys nodded. "Rugby," said Steve. He reached into his pocket and pulled out a flyer with the schedule on it. "Try and make it," he said to KC. "And if you do, come back to the locker room afterward. We always have a party."

"We *love* a good party," Eric agreed.

KC accepted the flyer. "Um, thank you for the invitation."

Mike punched Steve on the arm. "Come on," he said. "We've got practice."

Marielle waited until the two young men had gone. Then she turned to KC with a charming smile. "You see?" she asked. "You are definitely the girl most likely to get a date."

"Oh, come on," KC said. "They were talking to both of us."

"Oh no," Marielle insisted in a forced voice. "They only had eyes for you. You really must invite me over and show me what magic potion you drink every morning to mesmerize all the men on campus."

"It's nothing like that," KC said. "You're exaggerating."

"I'll tell you something else that's nice," Marielle said, "if you promise to keep it a secret."

KC was intrigued. "I'm very good at keeping secrets."

Marielle's voice once more lowered to a whisper. "I'm really not supposed to tell you yet. I'm sure Courtney wanted to tell you herself. . . ."

"Tell me what?" KC asked, leaning forward over the table. This was definitely sorority business and from the way Marielle sounded, it was good news.

"Promise me you'll act surprised when Courtney calls you," Marielle said.

KC nodded vigorously.

"Well . . ." Marielle pulled her chair closer to KC. "Courtney's going to invite you and two other potential pledges to the house for a special tea next week. It's to introduce you to all the other sisters. Of course, you'll still have to go through spring rush, but that's just a formality. All you have to do is make a good impression at the tea, and you're practically guaranteed a bid to join."

"Make a good impression?" KC asked. "What do I have to do?"

"It's easy," Marielle assured her. "All you have to do is answer some questions the sisters will ask you."

"What kind of questions?" KC asked. "Is it like a beauty pageant?"

Marielle laughed. "That's so precious! No, silly, they're not going to ask you if you're for world peace, or anything like that. The questions will be more personal, like what are your ambitions and your family . . . stuff like that."

"Oh." KC began to chew on a thumbnail. Her family? What could she possibly tell the sisters about her family that would impress them? Marielle's mother ran one of the biggest independent advertising agencies in Chicago, and Courtney Conner's father was chairman of a big Seattle bank. KC's parents ran a shabby health-food restaurant that struggled to get by. All KC could talk about was the time her mother had been making carrot juice and had forgotten to put the top on the juicer; little carrot shreds had shot out all over the restaurant, spraying everybody. She'd definitely have to be sketchy about her past. She could be a lot more detailed about the future, though. Future president or CEO of some large conglomerate, or maybe an independent financial consultant. That had a nice ring. And it was the truth.

KC couldn't depend on family money or connections to get her *anywhere*. At that point she couldn't depend on her grades, either. The only class she'd done well in the previous semester was Intro to Business. She'd gotten C's, barely, in everything else—not exactly a golden ticket into business school or a high-powered career. The sorority was her only chance of getting where she wanted to go. That was why she had to get in.

So why did she feel a lump in her stomach?

It wasn't the lemon meringue pie. KC vaguely felt that it had something to do with Winnie, or Peter Dvorsky, but she couldn't make the connection.

Four

·····················

"**P**ar-*ty*, par-*ty*, par-*ty!*"
Even through the closed door of her room, Melissa could hear the jocks making a ruckus downstairs in the lobby of Forest Hall. But for once she didn't need to wear Walkman headphones or earmuffs to screen out the noise. She was having no trouble at all concentrating on her biology chapter. In fact, homework had never been so much fun or so comfortable, thanks to the warm, firm cushion beneath her head. The cushion was Brooks's chest. The two of them lay on Melissa's bed.

Melissa sighed as she turned the page of her textbook. She felt so safe, so protected, so relaxed as she felt Brooks's peaceful breathing beneath her head. He was like a down comforter she could wrap around herself.

A snore from Brooks caused Melissa to sit up sharply. His political science notebook lay open over his face, and his chest rose and fell evenly. Smiling to herself, Melissa gently removed the notebook and closed it.

Brooks's eyes half opened. They were veiled by his thick blond lashes.

"Hello, sleepyhead," Melissa said, running her fingers lightly over his silky curls.

Brooks smiled, then pulled her down on top of him. Melissa giggled. She loved the feel of his sturdy arms inside the soft cotton of his rugby shirt.

"I guess we're not getting much work done," Brooks said.

"Speak for yourself," Melissa said. "I've read almost my entire biology chapter."

"Oh yeah?" Brooks said with interest. "Does that mean you're almost done for the evening?"

"Hardly," Melissa replied. "I've still got organic chemistry."

Brooks lowered Melissa gently to the bed, then propped himself up on one elbow. "Too bad," he said. "I guess you wouldn't be interested, then, in my great idea."

"What?" Melissa asked, reaching up to pull on one of Brooks's curls. When she let go, it bounced back to its original shape.

"No, no," Brooks said, shaking his head. "I wouldn't think of distracting you from your studies. I wouldn't even consider trying to drag you out of this sterile cinderblock cell of a room into the fresh air for an evening of fun. No, I wouldn't even suggest what I had in mind because I'm sure I'd only hear a swift and resounding no."

Melissa tried to look at Brooks sternly, but she was finding it difficult not to smile. "I knew you were up to no good by coming here tonight," she said. "Don't even try and tempt me. I have a will of iron and a lab test in three days."

Brooks pretended to look hurt. "I've already said I wouldn't."

"Then don't say another word," Melissa said, closing her eyes and pretending to be asleep.

Brooks placed an arm around Melissa and pulled her closer. "Just two words," he whispered in her ear. "Just let me say two words."

"It won't make a difference," Melissa said. "You can say whatever you want and I won't bend."

"Okay," Brooks said. He delicately lifted a strand

of Melissa's red hair away from her ear. "Testing. One, two, three. Can you hear me?"

Melissa suppressed a giggle. "Yes, I can hear you," she said. "Were those the words?"

"No, no. Here goes," said Brooks, his lips so near her ear she could feel his warm breath. "Miniature golf."

Melissa laughed. "Oh, you're right, Brooks," she said. "There were only two words in the entire world that would have lured me away from here, and those were them. Miniature golf. My favorite sport. How did you know?"

"But it's so much fun!" Brooks said. "And a new place just opened right near campus. We could walk it in ten minutes."

"Miniature golf?" Melissa said with a mocking expression on her face.

"This new place has *everything*," Brooks enthused. "Three separate courses: the Fairy Tale course, the Americana course, and the Goofball course. And each one has eighteen holes. There's never been anything like it!"

Melissa had to admit it sounded like fun. She'd only played once in her life—with her family, a long time ago, right before her father's drinking problem had gotten out of control. It had been fun trying to hit the brightly colored balls around alligators and helicopters and other ridiculous obstacles. But it was a weeknight, and Melissa really couldn't afford the time. She also wanted to get enough sleep so she'd be fresh for practice the next day.

"Maybe on Saturday," Melissa suggested. "I could take around two hours off, I guess."

"Now look," Brooks said, pulling back from her and looking her squarely in the eye. "Has there ever been a time when you didn't hand in a paper on time, ace a test, or show up for practice?"

"No," Melissa admitted.

"Have you or have you not discharged all your responsibilities throughout your life, whatever they might be?"

"That sounds like part of the wedding vow," Melissa said, giggling.

"Just answer my question," Brooks said seriously.

"Yes, I have," said Melissa, imitating his serious tone.

"And will two hours tonight take up any more time than two hours on Saturday?"

"No," said Melissa, weakening.

"I rest my case," said Brooks.

"I thought you were going to be an architect, not a lawyer," Melissa said.

"Just say yes," Brooks begged.

Melissa gazed up at his eyes, which looked so

eager, so hopeful. And why was she acting so stubborn? Brooks was right. She always got her work done. In fact, she was always working while everyone else was out having a good time. She couldn't even remember the last time she'd had fun. And where had it gotten her so far? Sure, she had good grades, but every night was the same, cooped up in a stuffy room with a textbook and a reading light. That wasn't living, was it? Besides, what harm could one night out do? Other people did it. It was time to join the human race.

Melissa hopped to her feet and grabbed her purple-and-gold windbreaker. "Let's go!" she said.

"Really?" Brooks asked. "I thought you liked to walk the straight and narrow."

"I can walk any way I want," Melissa said defiantly. "Or run."

A few minutes later, they had arrived at Springfield Tee-Time. The garishly painted sign was surrounded by flashing orange, red, and purple neon lights that cast a cheerful glow on the night sky and the surrounding trees. Beneath the sign was a little wooden shack painted red and white to resemble a barn. Behind the shack spread a vast field of Astroturf dotted with giant statues of Mickey Mouse, Bart Simpson, Teenage Mutant Ninja Turtles, Snow White, Alf, and the Muppets. A hot-pink windmill, with vanes that actually rotated, stood between a steamboat with a moving waterwheel and a giant wooden replica of a pinball machine. The huge lot was surrounded by a chain link fence.

"Didn't I tell you?" Brooks asked excitedly. "Is this the ultimate, or what?"

"It's so tacky!" Melissa exclaimed.

"That's why it's so great!" Brooks said. "Come on, let's get our clubs."

They walked up to the shack, where an overweight old man smoking a cigar sat behind a window, six sizes of golf clubs laid out on the counter before him.

"Two, please," said Brooks, handing the man ten dollars.

"Which course?" the man asked. "Fairy Tale, Americana, or Goofball?"

"You choose," Brooks said to Melissa.

"Well, I feel like a goofball just being here," Melissa began.

"Goofball," Brooks told the man.

The man handed Melissa a medium-length club and gave Brooks one that was slightly longer. "There's a bit of a crowd on that one," he said, "but the first tee is emptying out." He handed Brooks a card with a grid of boxes on it and a very short pencil with no eraser. "Please return your pencil when you're through," he said.

Clubs in hand, Melissa and Brooks passed under an archway labeled Goofball and approached the first tee, which was in front of a giant replica of Goofy, Mickey Mouse's dog.

"You want to go first?" Brooks asked.

"No, you go," Melissa said. "I like to come from behind."

"Oh!" said Brooks, raising his eyebrows. "Is this a competition?"

"Isn't everything?" Melissa asked, challenging Brooks with her stare.

"Okay," Brooks said. "You want to play tough, then we have to play for stakes."

"Name it," Melissa said.

"Loser has to eat a double-fudge sundae with gooey strawberry sauce and whipped cream. Tonight at the snack bar."

"No way!" Melissa complained. "I'm in training!"

"Oh," Brooks teased. "Do you expect to lose?"

"Of course not," Melissa said, assuming the same confident attitude with which she approached her races. "But I won't have the time to sit with you when *you* lose."

"You won't have to," Brooks bargained. "If I lose, I'll go by myself."

"It's a deal," Melissa agreed. "Golfers, take your marks!"

Brooks placed his purple golf ball on the scruffy green surface and spread his feet wide. He swung his club gently back and forth a few times, stopping right before he hit the ball. Then he swung his club way back.

"Eat this, Goofy!" Brooks cried as his club connected solidly with the ball. The purple ball flew through the air, hit Goofy, and bounced several times on the green, ending up next to the dog.

"I guess Goofy wasn't hungry," Melissa jibed. Placing her bright yellow ball on the green, she closed her eyes and breathed. *Inhale, two, three, four. Exhale, two, three, four.* Melissa swung and connected. The ball flew neatly up Goofy's tongue and into his mouth. "Good job!" Brooks said, hugging her and kissing her on the cheek as the ball rolled out of Goofy and into the metal cup. "You got a hole in one!"

"You're not supposed to be happy for me," Melissa said.

"Why not?" Brooks asked.

"Because I'm beating you."

Brooks grew thoughtful. "Oh."

"What's the matter?" Melissa asked. "Am I being too intense about this? I mean, I know I said it was going to be a competition, but it really is just a friendly game. Is that what's bothering you?"

"No," Brooks said. "I like that you're competitive. You're tough and independent. My ex-girlfriend . . ." He trailed off, then grew silent.

"Faith." Melissa supplied the name. "You can say it. What about Faith?"

"Well, she wasn't as independent as you are," Brooks said. "At least while we were in high school. And that made me too overprotective. I'm sure that's what destroyed our relationship."

"It wasn't just your fault," Melissa said. "People change. People move on. You can't blame yourself for that."

"No, but you know yourself that I have a tendency to come on too strong. But with you, I think it's easier for me to back off because you have so much strength of your own."

"Thank you," Melissa said.

"Excuse me," said a female voice.

Melissa and Brooks turned to see a young woman with two blond children who were impatiently swinging their tiny golf clubs at each other's feet.

"Are you done with this tee?" she asked.

"I am," Melissa said, poking Brooks playfully in the ribs. "But he needs a few more strokes. We'll be off in a minute." Melissa sprinted around Goofy and retrieved her ball from the hole.

Brooks finally made it on his fourth stroke, and they moved on to the next tee. A giant sneaker tapped its toe up and down in the center of a straightaway, alternately blocking and unblocking the path to the hole. They couldn't get on right away because a family of six still crowded the green.

"Does it still hurt?" Melissa asked as they watched a toddler blatantly cheat by dragging his ball to the hole with his club. No one in his family seemed to mind.

"Does what hurt?" Brooks asked.

"The breakup with Faith," Melissa said. "I guess you still miss her."

"Sometimes I do," Brooks admitted, "but that's not the part that bothers me. It's definitely over between us. It was just the *way* we broke up. It was so sudden. I mean, one day we were doing great, the next day she was saying goodbye. It felt like somebody punched me in the stomach when I wasn't looking."

"I know how that feels," Melissa said sympathetically. "Almost every relationship I've ever had has been a big disappointment."

"Of course, when I think about it now," Brooks went on, "the breakup was a long time in coming. I must have been getting on Faith's nerves for months, years even. I was smothering her, but neither one of us realized it until we got to Springfield."

"Well, at least you learned something," Melissa said philosophically. "I mean, I can tell you're really trying to tone yourself down with me, and I appreciate it."

"Do you really think so?" Brooks asked. "Do you really see a difference?"

"Yes," Melissa said. "For example, you really overdid it with the flowers and soup and everything the time I was sick, but you're a lot better now."

"I hope you mean that," Brooks said, "because I'm so afraid . . ." He turned away from her and a worry line appeared on his forehead.

"What are you afraid of?" Melissa asked. "You can tell me."

Brooks turned back and looked at her intently. "I'm afraid of getting hurt again," he said. "I'm afraid of not reading the signals right, the way I did with Faith. I can't go through that again. It's just too painful."

"I won't hurt you," Melissa promised.

"That's what you say now," Brooks said, "but you might feel different later on. And if you do, promise me one thing."

"What?" Melissa asked.

Brooks grabbed her by both arms and looked at her intently. "If you ever want to break up with me, tell me right away. Don't dangle me along while you're making up your mind. Don't fill me with false hope. Tell me what I did wrong, and end it. Cleanly. Will you do that? *Will you do that?*"

"Why are you so sure *you're* the one who's going to do something wrong?" Melissa said. "I'm not perfect."

"You're not?" Brooks asked in mock surprise. "I thought perfection is what you're always striving for."

"Well, it is," Melissa said seriously. "And I'm almost there. But even I have a little way to go."

When Brooks looked at Melissa as if he believed her, she burst out laughing.

"I'm kidding!" she said.

Brooks sighed. "Just remember your promise, okay? No surprises."

"Except this one," Melissa said, throwing her arms around him and kissing him long and hard on the lips, pressing her body against his.

"Wow," Brooks said softly when she'd finally pulled back. "You've never done that before. I mean, you're not usually that physical."

"I'm doing a lot of things tonight that I've never

done before," Melissa said. "And I like it. I like it a lot."

"So do I!" Brooks leaned down to kiss her again.

When they looked up, the large family ahead of them had finally moved on to the third tee. Brooks took his starting position on the green and stared menacingly at the giant sneaker. "Feets don't fail me now," he sang.

Melissa laughed and tossed her golf club aside. Then she cozied up behind Brooks. "Here," she said, placing her arms around him and gripping his club right beneath his hands. "I think you need a little help with your swing."

"You got that right," Brooks said, turning his head and smiling.

At the end of the round, Melissa had beaten Brooks by seventeen points *and* won a free game, for which she had taken a rain check. "You're not really going to let me eat alone," Brooks pleaded as the two trudged back to campus.

"I don't know," Melissa teased him. "A deal's a deal."

Brooks pouted. "Fine. I'll just eat myself into oblivion and get so fat they'll have to build a new dorm just for me."

Melissa laughed. "I really had fun tonight," she said. "Believe it or not, there were actually stretches of time when I forgot about work completely. Whole minutes, even. I can't remember the last time I felt so happy."

"Does this mean you'll sit with me?" Brooks asked.

"Only if you give me a ride to the snack bar."

"A ride?" Brooks asked. "I don't have a car."

"But you have a back," Melissa said, running her hands over his shoulders. "A nice strong back."

"Are you asking for a piggyback ride?"

"You got it," Melissa answered. "I'm tired of getting everywhere on my own steam."

"Hop on!" Brooks said, leaning forward.

Melissa jumped up and wrapped her legs around Brooks's waist. "Giddyap!" she commanded him, playfully slapping his side.

Brooks pretended to neigh. "Double-fudge sundae with strawberry sauce and whipped cream, here we come!"

"Wait! Wait a minute," Melissa began. "I didn't say I'd eat—" But Brooks was off and running.

Several minutes later, they sat very close together, the double-fudge sundae between them.

"I should really have tied you up outside with a bag of oats," Melissa said, stroking his neck. "Ice cream's too good for horses."

"Even very *good* horses?" Brooks asked.

"Well, maybe I'll let you have a taste," Melissa said. "But I certainly don't need it at this hour. You're really a bad influence on me, Baldwin."

"Thank you," Brooks said, spooning fudge ice cream into her mouth. "So tell me," he said more seriously, "what did you mean before when you said that all your relationships were big disappointments? Did you mean with boyfriends?"

"No," Melissa admitted. "I've been too busy to get involved before now. I was thinking more about my family."

"You hardly ever talk about them," Brooks said.

"I try to avoid the subject whenever possible," Melissa said, "although I've already told you more than I've ever told anyone."

"Has your father always been . . . sick?" Brooks asked.

"It's funny," Melissa said. "That's the same word he and my mother have always used, and I guess it's not wrong since alcoholism is a disease. But he's never admitted he had a problem. It didn't get really bad until I was about ten or so. Before that, he held down a job—not that it was anything spectacular. He was a night watchman at a hotel in Springfield. He hasn't done anything for the past eight years, though. He hardly ever leaves the house. My mother supports us."

"You said she was a housekeeper?"

Melissa nodded. "She's worked the past ten years for the same family. She's there every day except Sunday."

"Which means you didn't see her much when you were growing up," Brooks observed.

"No." Melissa sighed. "She spent most of her time raising someone else's kids. I think that's why my brother turned out the way he did."

"Didn't you say he was in a band?" Brooks asked.

"If you could call it that," Melissa said. "It's really just a group of guys from the neighborhood. They don't play anything original; they're just a cover band, and most of it is heavy metal. I really worry about him. When he's not playing, he's just sitting around the house with my father. It wouldn't surprise me if he turned into an alcoholic, too."

Brooks took Melissa's hand and held it comfortingly. She sighed. With Brooks so warm and near, it was almost possible to pretend that none of her family life was real. It was just a story she was telling. Reality was her and Brooks sitting together, eating ice cream, with a bright future to look forward to.

"Thank you," Melissa said.

"For what?"

"For listening and not making me feel as if I'm a

freak. I know my family's not exactly something to be proud of, but you've made me feel that's okay."

"Of course it's okay," Brooks reassured her, squeezing her hand. "They are who they are. No one's family is perfect."

"Not even yours?" Melissa asked. "Somehow I always pictured you coming from one of those 1950s families, like the one in *Father Knows Best,* because you're so well adjusted."

Brooks laughed. "You know my parents are divorced."

"But you and your dad and stepmother seemed so happy over Thanksgiving that I forgot. I guess the divorce was hard, though."

Brooks shrugged. "It was a long time ago, and it was really cordial. I mean, my parents still call each other up to say hello. They and their new spouses even socialize together."

"That's weird," Melissa said. "I mean, it's unusual. Don't they feel any bitterness?"

"Not really," Brooks said. "They were high-school sweethearts who got married too young. Then they both started changing, and it just wasn't right anymore. But they still liked each other as friends."

"Sounds like you and Faith," Melissa said.

Brooks nodded. "I guess it's better to do most of

your changing *before* you get married. Not that you ever completely stop."

"Do you like your stepmother?" Melissa asked.

"A lot," Brooks said. "My parents let me choose who I wanted to live with, and I chose my dad. My stepmother's been really good to me. She always treated me like her own child."

"So it wasn't too traumatic, considering."

"Nope."

A white-uniformed busboy pushed a broom past them and said, "Sorry, but I've got to kick you out of here. We're closing."

Melissa suddenly noticed that they were the only students left in the snack bar except for the busboy and two waiters stacking chairs on top of tables. She looked at her watch. "Two o'clock!" she exclaimed. "I can't believe how long we've been sitting here."

Brooks smiled and took her hand. "I'll walk you back to your dorm."

Melissa let herself in quietly. She was careful not to disturb Winnie, who lay sprawled diagonally across her bed, one arm dangling over the side, her hand resting inside one of her jingle-bell boots. Melissa smiled to herself, thinking how odd it was that *she* should be the one coming home late while Winnie was the one sleeping. Not even bothering to put on her pajamas, Melissa stripped to her underpants and a T-shirt and crawled under the covers. The clock said 2:37. She'd wasted an entire evening, and she was getting to bed four hours past her bedtime.

Melissa had never felt so good in her entire life.

Five

"Today we shall discuss the European Age in world history," began Professor Hermann, lifting his bifocals from the podium and placing them low on the bridge of his nose. "It is an age characterized by uninterrupted and exploitative interference by Europeans with the domestic affairs of other peoples."

Faith scribbled industriously in her notebook, trying not to miss a word of the Western Civ lecture, but she kept turning her head to look at the door.

"Are you sure you haven't seen Winnie?" Faith whispered to KC, who sat to her left, alternately taking notes and highlighting with a hot-pink magic marker.

"Shhhh!" KC said. "I'm trying to concentrate."

Faith turned to Lauren, on her right. "I wonder where Winnie is."

"She'll show up," Lauren assured her. "She probably overslept."

"During the Middle Ages," Professor Hermann continued from behind the podium at the bottom of the large amphitheater, "individual Europeans had made journeys deep into the Sahara, and Marco Polo was only the most famous of the many who had made contact with the Far East. . . ."

Faith tried to concentrate, as several hundred of her classmates were doing, but she kept worrying about Winnie. Winnie had been doing so well first semester. Her grades had been good and she'd finally settled down with one guy, Josh Gaffey, a computer genius who lived down the hall.

Then Travis Bennett, the guy she'd met in Paris, reappeared, and things started going haywire again. Winnie couldn't give up either one, so she'd gone out with both until KC spilled the beans. Ever since then, Winnie had really gone off the deep end. She'd been cutting classes even more than she'd done in high school, she'd spent an entire week living on nothing but nacho-cheese Doritos and Host-

ess chocolate cupcakes, and her outfits, always out-
rageous, had become downright scary-looking. She
almost looked like a bag lady, layering five and six
shirts on top of one another to keep out the "freezing emptiness of the cosmos," as she put it.

Faith was afraid of what Winnie was going to do
next.

"You're not taking any notes!" Lauren hissed,
pointing at the empty page in Faith's notebook.

"I'm worried because Winnie's still not here,"
Faith whispered back. "I hope she hasn't done anything crazy."

"You mean *more* crazy," KC whispered, highlighting a line of notes with her marker.

"Try and be a little understanding," Faith
snapped at KC. "What if she's hurt, like at Thanksgiving? We thought she was just being flakey, but
she was actually in the hospital with a head injury."

"I'm sure she's fine. At this very moment she's
probably mooning over some new guy with a Mo-
hawk haircut and a safety pin stuck in his nose.
Maybe he offered to take her for a ride on his mo-
torcycle."

"Shhhhhh!" said a girl behind them. "I'm trying
to listen to the lecture!"

"Sorry," Faith said. She uncapped her pen, but
she didn't take notes with it. She stuck the plastic

cap in her mouth and began to chew on it nervously. The way Winnie had been acting lately had to be a cry for help. Faith had heard the cry and was willing to do anything she could, but she wasn't sure if Winnie knew that.

". . . the voyagers encountered a Japan recovering from civil war, a China that had turned in on itself, an Indian coast divided among small powers who could be set one against the other, and an Incan empire confused by a succession crisis." Professor Hermann lifted his stack of notes from the podium, straightened them, and put them in a folder. "That concludes today's lecture. For next time, we will go back to the Renaissance."

Faith looked around in surprise. Had she really been so preoccupied with Winnie that she had missed the entire lecture? On either side of her, her friends were closing their notebooks, and Winnie still hadn't arrived.

"I think we should go find Winnie," Faith said worriedly. "Right now."

"I'm sure she's fine," KC said, loading her books into her briefcase and snapping it shut. "She's just a little depressed, that's all. I guarantee you, she's in one piece."

"I won't feel better until I see for myself," Faith

insisted. "Let's go over to her dorm to make sure she's okay."

"I don't have time," KC said. "I've got accounting."

"That's not for two hours," Faith said. "Couldn't you pop your head in, just for a minute? I'm sure it would mean a lot to Winnie."

"Sorry," said KC, picking up her briefcase and rising from her chair. "I've got some reading to catch up on before class."

Before Faith could plead with her further, KC was in the aisle, climbing the stairs to the back of the classroom.

"I'll go with you," Lauren offered. "I've got an interview at the recycling center, but it's not for an hour."

Faith gave Lauren a grateful smile.

Drip! . . . drip! . . . drip! . . .
That was the only sound Faith heard as she and Lauren entered the lobby of Forest Hall. For once there were no stereos blasting, no plopping sounds as water balloons were dropped down stairwells, no warlike yells as opposing teams played football in the narrow hallway.

There was just the dripping sound, regular and steady, like water hitting the floor. At least, Faith hoped that it was water. What if it were something else . . . like blood? What if Winnie had fallen and hit her head?

Faith took off down the hall in the direction of the sound. Lauren followed, though she didn't understand why Faith was running.

When she saw the stain on the hall floor, Faith stopped short and Lauren skidded into her.

"What's the matter?" Lauren asked, her voice muffled by the fringes of Faith's suede jacket.

Faith pointed to the beige carpet. A small round stain dotted the floor. A few inches away was another stain, then another, and another, forming a trail down the hall.

"What is it?" Lauren asked.

Faith knelt down on the floor to get a closer look. Then she breathed a sigh of relief. "It's not red," she said happily. "It's purple. Maybe someone's painting in their room."

Heads down, the two girls followed the trail of purple dots down the hall, into the bathroom, and up to a pair of familiar-looking boots with jingle bells on them.

"Winnie!" Faith exclaimed, looking up. What she saw made her exclaim even more loudly. *"Winnie! What have you done to yourself?"*

Winnie Gottlieb stood at the sink wearing nothing but a pair of neon green satin shorts, her jingle-bell boots, and a tan rain poncho. But it wasn't her outfit that was so incredible. It was her hair. Usually dark brown and spiky, it was now a vivid shade of purple. Still wet, the dye was dripping down the back and sides of her poncho and hitting the floor with wet plops, forming an ever-growing purple puddle.

"Do you like it?" Winnie asked, grinning.

"It's purple!" Lauren exclaimed, her jaw hanging open.

"No, it's not. It's fuschia," Winnie corrected her. "Purple's got more blue in it. This is closer to a hot pink, actually." Winnie boosted herself up on the sink, balancing on the rim of the basin with her knees so she could get a closer look at herself in the mirror. "Yup," she said. "Definitely fuschia."

"Why, Winnie?" Faith asked. "Why did you do it?"

Winnie looked hurt. "Why not? I've got nothing better to do." Winnie looked down at the floor, then back at the sink. "Hey, it's sort of fun up here," she said. "Hmm, I wonder . . ." Holding onto the shelf at the base of the mirror, Winnie placed one jingle-belled boot on the edge of the sink, then the other, so that she was squatting on the soles of her feet. Then, slowly, carefully, she stood up.

"I can do it!" she cried, her head up near the ceiling. "I'm a tightrope walker! Watch this!"

With one hand touching the wall for balance, Winnie reached one foot forward toward the next sink.

"Come down from there!" Faith pleaded with her. "You don't know if those sinks will support your weight."

"Yeah!" Lauren chimed in. "What if one of them breaks off the wall while you're on it? There could be a flood in here."

"Après moi, le deluge," Winnie said. "I learned that in Paris."

"What does that mean?" Faith asked, moving alongside the row of sinks so she could catch Winnie if she fell.

"It means, 'After me, the flood,'" Winnie explained. "One of the King Louises said it, I think."

"Please, please come down from there," Faith said as Winnie reached the last sink in the row.

Winnie lowered herself, but she didn't get off the sink. She sat in it, swinging her jingling boots like a little girl in a chair that was too big for her.

"We missed you in Western Civ," Lauren said,

trying to act as if this was just a normal conversation.

"Yes," Faith said. "Why weren't you in class?"

Winnie shook her head. "You two obviously don't understand," she said. "We're not in college to read books and take tests. Do you think we're going to remember any of this stuff twenty years from now? No, we're really here to learn about ourselves and form relationships with other people, and since I've already failed at that, there's no point in my going to classes."

"You haven't failed, Winnie," Faith said, placing a comforting hand on Winnie's bare, purple-splotched arm. "You're just having a difficult time right now."

Winnie yanked her arm away and started playing with her hair, twisting her spikes to make them stand up even straighter. "I *have* failed," she said matter-of-factly. "Everyone's abandoned me. It's got to be more than a coincidence that everyone who's ever known me has decided I'm not worth knowing."

"That's not true, Winnie," Lauren said. "I like you a lot."

"Then you're a fool," Winnie said. "I wrecked your beautiful, expensive car, and if it weren't for me you could have sold it and lived off the money instead of slaving away in that hotel."

"It's really not that bad," Lauren said, "and I don't hold the accident against you." Faith was silently grateful for that. Lauren had lent Winnie her BMW the night Winnie was supposed to break up with Travis at the Beanery. On her way back, Winnie had been hit by a driver with no insurance. At the same time, Lauren's mother had canceled her insurance on the BMW, and Lauren had been left with nothing.

"And what about you, Faith?" Winnie said, turning to her friend with glistening eyes. "I don't think I saw you for a total of ten minutes while you were directing *Alice in Wonderland*. You must have been avoiding me."

"Of course I wasn't," Faith said. "I was just very busy, and even so we still spent *some* time together."

"What about KC?" Winnie continued. "She doesn't even speak to me anymore. She must think I'm a horrible person after I cheated on Travis and Josh *and* pushed her in the pool during Winter Formal. What kind of friend was I to do that? I knew she wanted to win more than anything in the world, and I deliberately ruined her chances."

"But—" Faith began, but Winnie was on a roll and there was no stopping her.

"And Josh and Travis," Winnie said. "You don't even have to tell me I'm an idiot for letting both of them slip away. I was the luckiest girl in the world to have not one but two fabulous guys in love with me, and what did I do? I screwed up both relationships and drove both guys away. They both seemed quite happy to go, by the way. Maybe neither of them ever really loved me to begin with. Maybe I'm just inherently unlovable and no one's had the nerve to tell me. I guess I understand, though. I mean, how can a person go on living when they confront a truth like that?"

"It's not a truth," Faith said, pulling at a metal button on her denim skirt. "It's just a figment of your imagination because you're very upset right now. There are a lot of people who love you, even Travis and Josh, and if you weren't ready to choose one of them, you weren't ready. Everybody has to do things in their own time."

While Faith was speaking, Lauren had quietly gone to a paper-towel dispenser at the end of the row of sinks and removed a fat stack of towels. "Let's clean you up and get you back to your room," she said to Winnie.

"Oh no," Winnie wailed, covering her eyes. "I don't think I can leave the bathroom looking like this. What if Josh sees me? That's the last thing I need. Then he'll know how lucky he was to get away from me."

"Maybe we could rinse the purple out," Faith suggested. "Does it come out when you shampoo?"

Winnie shook her head glumly. "It's permanent. Here to stay, at least until my hair grows out."

"Okay," said Faith calmly. "Then we'll just have to do the best we can."

Faith took some towels from Lauren, wet them, and started mopping up the floor while Lauren dried Winnie's hair. Then they both started cleaning off Winnie's poncho. All the while, Faith was frantically trying to figure out what she could do to help with Winnie's bigger problems.

"There," said Faith finally. "Now let's dash across the hall to your room really quick. I'm sure no one will see us. Come on, Lauren. Let's flank her on either side. We'll make a Winnie sandwich."

Their shoulders pressed together, the three left the bathroom and walked swiftly down the hall. Suddenly Winnie froze.

Faith and Lauren stopped, too, when they saw what Winnie saw. A tall, slim young man with long dark hair was coming toward them down the hall. His oversized T-shirt hung outside his faded jeans, and he wore a woven bracelet around his wrist. It was Josh Gaffey. Even worse, walking next to him was a tall, preppy-looking blond girl who was smiling at him as if he was the cutest guy she'd ever seen.

Faith looked back at Winnie, nervous about what she might do. Winnie's eyes grew wider and wider. Then suddenly she threw herself against the wall, careened across the hall, and crashed into the other wall. Back and forth she went while Josh, the blond, Faith, and Lauren stared.

"You happy now, Josh?" Winnie asked. "I'm bouncing off the walls. They're probably going to straitjacket me and take me away, right, Faith?"

As Winnie careened back and forth, Faith tried to smile at Josh and the girl as if this were some big joke. Josh looked at Winnie with concern, but the blond girl grabbed his arm and pulled him inside his room.

Without another word, Winnie turned around and ran back to the bathroom, slamming the door shut behind her. Faith and Lauren tried to open it, but it was locked.

"Come on, Winnie!" Faith cried, leaning her head against the door. "You can't stay in there all day. And people are going to have to use the bathroom. You can't keep the door locked."

There was no answer.

"Winnie!" Lauren pleaded. "Come out! The

worst is over. Staying in the bathroom won't do any good."

Faith was sure she heard sobbing behind the door. "We have to do something," she said.

"But she won't listen to us," Lauren said. "Who else could talk to her?"

An answer came immediately to Faith's mind: Melissa McDormand, Winnie's roommate. Though Melissa and Winnie hadn't gotten along too well in the beginning, they had eventually become good friends. And Winnie hadn't included Melissa in her list of people who had abandoned her. Maybe Winnie would listen to her. Melissa did seem like an extremely sensible, level-headed person.

Faith felt very uncomfortable at the thought of talking to Melissa, but Winnie was in desperate trouble. Faith had to push her personal problems aside.

The crying inside the bathroom grew louder.

"Are you all right, Winnie?" Faith shouted.

"I'm fine!" Winnie screamed.

There was only one thing Faith could do. She had to talk to Melissa right away.

"Stay here," Faith told Lauren. "Try and talk to her. I'll be right back."

Faith dashed down the hall and pounded on Winnie's door. There was no answer. Melissa had to be home! Faith knocked again louder. That time she heard footsteps. Faith swallowed hard as the door opened.

Melissa stood with her hand on the doorknob, a pair of Walkman headphones covering her ears. "What's up?" she asked bluntly.

Faith took a deep breath. "Winnie's in trouble," she said. "She's locked herself in the bathroom and won't come out."

Without a word, Melissa removed the headphones and placed them on her desk. Then she turned to face Faith. "What can I do?" she asked.

Faith shook her head. "I wish I knew. She's really hysterical right now. She dyed her hair purple and then Josh saw her in the hall and he was with another girl, and now Winnie's crying and she won't even talk to us. She thinks everyone's abandoned her."

"That's ridiculous," Melissa said.

"I know," Faith said, "but I don't think Winnie knows that. I wish there were some way we could prove to her that we love her."

"Maybe we could take her out or something," Melissa suggested. "She's been saying she wants to check out that bowling alley with the bar that serves the green milkshakes. Not that that solves our immediate problem. I'll try and talk to her if you think that will get her out of the bathroom."

"It might," Faith said, "although, now that I think about it, she'll have to come out eventually. She'll either get hungry or someone will want to take a shower. But I like your suggestion about taking her out." Faith thought for a moment. "I have an even better idea! It's Winnie's eighteenth birthday next week."

"That's right," Melissa said. "She mentioned it. The big one-eight."

"What if we threw her a surprise party?" Faith asked. "If you and Lauren help me, we could do it up really special. I'll make sure KC shows up, and we'll invite a whole bunch of other people, too, so she knows how much we care."

"It's a good idea," Melissa said. "I'm pretty busy, but I'll do what I can."

"Great!" Faith said. "I'll, um, call you." She felt awkward again. But she thought about how happy Winnie would feel when she was surrounded by all her friends and how happy she herself would feel if KC and Winnie got over their fight. Yes, a surprise party was just the thing, and if it meant including Melissa, then that was the way it had to be.

"What about right now, though?" she asked Melissa.

Melissa looked hard at Faith. "It looks like you're worn out just thinking about this," she said. "Why don't you go on home? I'll talk to Winnie."

"You will? That's great! I mean, I love Winnie, but . . ."

"Hey, I live with her, remember?"

Faith smiled. "Right. Thanks again." As she left Forest Hall, she was beginning to understand why Brooks seemed to care so much for this serious, intense girl. At least she could thank Brooks for not replacing her with a total dweeb.

Six

Lauren raced across the campus green toward the recycling center. She'd left poor Winnie behind her at Forest Hall, but she was already late for her interview at the recycling center.

"Lauren!"

In the distance, Lauren saw Dash sitting on the front steps of the center, waving to her.

"Hurry up!" he cried. *"We're late!"*

Lauren purposely slowed down. Let him wait. He deserved it for not telling her the truth about his family coming to visit.

"Sorry," said Lauren primly as she walked right past him up the steps.

"Hey!" Dash said, spinning her around to face him. He placed one arm firmly behind her back and pulled her close, as if he were about to dance with her. "Is that any way to greet me? We haven't seen each other for *hours.*"

Lauren closed her eyes, trying to ignore the pleasure she felt at being so close to him. She reveled in the leathery smell and buttery feel of his jacket, the firmness of his muscles pressing against her softer flesh. "Hi," she said softly. She wanted to sound angry, but she just couldn't do it. She was too happy being in his arms.

"Come on," Dash said, pushing open the door to the recycling center. "Mr. DiStanislao's waiting inside. I didn't ask him any questions, though, since I knew you'd kill me if I did."

"Good job, partner," Dash said as they left the recycling center a half-hour later. "It's not the same as the frat story, but it's the kind of stuff people on campus need to know."

Lauren trotted along beside him. "We did pretty well."

"I think we got enough information in there for three stories," Dash enthused.

"Maybe we could do a series," Lauren said. "One piece each week, covering different aspects of recycling, biodegradability . . ."

"We could get the center page," Dash said, continuing the thought. "You know, something our readers could take out of the paper and save as a resource. We could tell them about the recycling program on campus, give them the lowdown on which products are really biodegradable and which aren't."

Lauren nodded. "If we got even half the students on campus to change their habits, that would be thousands of pounds of garbage kept out of landfills every week."

"We have a mission!" Dash cried. "And together we'll get the message out there." In his enthusiasm, he had walked right past Lauren, not noticing that she had lagged behind. "What's the matter?" he asked, going back to meet her. "Did you lose something?"

My confidence in this relationship, Lauren wanted to answer. How could she feel good about him, about them, when he was keeping secrets? She desperately wanted to ask him about his parents' visit, but she was afraid to admit she'd read his mail.

Dash planted himself directly in front of Lauren, his legs spread wide. "Something is bothering you and you're not taking another step until you tell me what it is."

"I can't talk about it," Lauren said, hanging her head.

Dash placed one finger beneath her chin and gently raised it so she had to look in his eyes. "You *can*," he insisted. "You can tell me anything."

"You'll have a fit," Lauren said.

"I promise I won't."

"No matter what?"

"Unless you murdered someone. Just kidding," Dash said, looking tenderly into her eyes. "Go ahead."

Lauren couldn't meet Dash's eyes when she said, "I read your letter."

"Which one?" Dash asked, confused. "We got so many on that hazing article—"

"No," Lauren cut in. "The pink one. From your mother."

"Oh." Dash's olive skin paled. "But you couldn't understand it, could you? You don't speak Spanish."

"I understood enough," Lauren said. "Mama, Papa, Anna. Moreno's. Seven-thirty. Sabado. That's Saturday, isn't it? Why didn't you tell me your family is coming? Why don't you want me to meet them?"

"I never said that!" Dash said. "Of course I want

you to meet them . . . next time they come. But you misunderstood the letter. They were already here. It was *last* Saturday, not *this* Saturday."

Lauren knew Dash was lying. The letter had been dated two days after Dash said the visit had taken place. She decided to take another tack.

"Will you at least tell me about them?" she asked.

"There's not much to tell," Dash mumbled.

"What's that?" Lauren asked. "I couldn't hear you."

"I said they're just your basic family."

"What does your dad do?" Lauren asked.

"He's got a steady job," Dash said. "Nothing worth going into." Dash seemed embarrassed, unwilling to elaborate.

"Does your mother work?" Lauren asked.

"Oh, yes," Dash said. "You know, the cost of living's very high. They can really use the two incomes."

"What does she do?" Lauren asked.

"She works in a hospital."

"Is she a nurse?"

"No . . . her job's not really medical. It's more like paperwork. Do you mind if we change the subject?"

Did Dash really still see Lauren as a sorority snob who looked down on secretarial work?

"Okay," Lauren said. "How about your sister?"

"Anna . . . well . . . you might say she's involved with the law." Dash checked his watch. "Ten to three," he said briskly. "Editors' meeting in ten minutes. I can't be late again or they'll have my head on a platter. Look, I'll call you later, okay?" Giving her a quick kiss on the cheek, Dash took off across the green.

Lauren's head was swimming. From the sound of it, Dash came from a very troubled family, or at least a poor one. Was he too ashamed of his parents and sister to introduce them to his girlfriend?

An even more troubling, frightening thought came to Lauren's mind. Maybe Dash's family were a group of hard-working immigrants who'd resent their son taking up with an educated girl from the upper classes—a pudgy, nearsighted girl who'd been kicked out of her own family. Lauren's stomach constricted with a sickening squeeze. That was the real reason Dash didn't want Lauren to meet his family. He wasn't embarrassed by them; he was embarrassed by *her*.

"Hey, class is over."

Melissa, whose chin had been resting on the palm of her hand, looked up dreamily. "Hmm?"

A guy towering over her gestured to the rapidly

emptying lecture hall. "It's time to go," he said. "You don't want the janitor to lock you in."

"Oh," Melissa said, her eyes finally focusing on the face far above. "Thanks. I'll be going in a minute."

The guy shrugged and climbed over her with his long legs to get into the main aisle.

Melissa was thinking again about Brooks. She could still feel the solidity of his back and the gentle rocking motion as he had carried her back to campus. She could still taste the sweetness of his lips, sticky with ice cream, as he kissed her goodnight. She'd never experienced this fuzzy-headed morning-after-a-romantic-evening feeling before, and she almost didn't want it to end. It was like proof that the night before had been real.

Melissa threw her books in her knapsack and headed for the gym. At the entrance, she flashed her student ID card at the guard in the glass booth. Then she pushed through the turnstile, heading for the basement locker room.

When she got to her locker, Melissa noticed Caitlin Bruneau, already dressed, sitting on a bench at the end of the row. Caitlin was speaking quietly to Demi Smith, a junior who was one of the track team's best hurdlers. Demi wore her long hair in cornrow braids, which she then pulled back into a neat ponytail. Demi looked up when Melissa came in, and Caitlin turned around.

"Look who's here! You ready to pump some iron?"

Melissa nodded. "Terry wants me to work hamstrings today. He says if I build the muscles around the hamstring, it will lessen my chance of getting injured again."

"I hear you," Demi said, placing her hands on her powerful thighs. "I think I pull mine once a year."

"I haven't yet, knockwood," Caitlin said, rapping on her head. "I think if you keep a positive attitude, you can avoid injury."

Demi laughed. "You've just been lucky, that's all." She got up off the bench and headed for the entrance to the weight room, with Caitlin close behind. Melissa, now dressed in sweatpants and a T-shirt, followed.

"Legs!" Terry exclaimed as the three girls entered. Melissa looked from Caitlin to Demi, not sure what he was talking about. "Legs McDormand!" Terry repeated. "My rising star!"

Caitlin poked Melissa in the ribs. "Watch out," she said. "He called you Legs. We all know what happens after that."

"What?" asked Melissa fearfully.

"You're marked," Caitlin said dramatically. "Now that Terry's discovered you, he's going to work you until you're just a tiny heap of bones and sinew."

Demi rolled her eyes at Caitlin. "Now what are you trying to scare the girl for?"

"It's true, isn't it?" Caitlin said. "Remember *our* freshman year?"

Terry came down the aisle between the machines and put his arm around Melissa's shoulders. "You ready to work?" he asked.

"Good luck, Legs!" Caitlin giggled as she and Demi went to join the other girls already sweating and straining.

"Get back here, Bruneau," Terry said, stopping Caitlin. "I've got a special program in mind for the two of you today."

Caitlin shrugged. "What's up?"

"I want you two to team up today, go through the machines together, starting with upper body. We'll get quads and hamstrings at the end."

Caitlin hopped up onto the pull-down machine. "Is this a contest?" she asked the coach. "Or do you want Melissa to observe my flawless technique and learn from a master?"

"I think you can make each other better," said Terry. "Okay, how many pounds you got?"

Caitlin turned around to see how many metal

plates were stacked above the pin. "Ninety," she said.

"It's a start," Terry said. "Go ahead. Give me a set."

Caitlin sat on the bench and pulled down on the overhead bar. "One!" she counted. "Two . . ."

As Caitlin counted, Terry said to Melissa, "I like what I've been seeing out there, McDormand. You've got every natural gift a runner could ask for, and the mind to back it up. If you keep working, getting stronger, I think you could shave at least another second off your time and win the eight hundred next time."

"If I let her," Caitlin said from the lat machine. "And I might not be in the mood. Seven . . . eight . . ."

Terry winked at Caitlin, then went on. "It's important to strengthen your upper body so you can use your arms to pump even as your legs are giving out. You have to use everything you've got."

". . . twelve!" Caitlin finished, jumping down off the machine. "Your turn, Legs! You want me to make it lighter for you?"

Melissa laughed. "Throw on another plate," she said. "I don't want to waste my time on *wimp* weight."

Caitlin made a face. "It's your funeral," she said.

Melissa took her position and pulled down on the overhead bar. It felt much heavier than usual. Had Caitlin added more than one plate?

"How much weight is this?" asked Melissa. "One ten? One twenty?"

"What's the matter, McDormand?" Caitlin asked. "Are your eyes bigger than your muscles? It's one hundred ten. Terry can confirm it if you don't believe me."

"One ten," Terry said. He checked his clipboard. "What's the matter, McDormand? You did one ten last time."

"No problem," Melissa said as she strained against the bar. "One!" she counted, trying not to let the strain show. "Two . . ."

"What's the matter, McDormand?" Caitlin asked. "Feeling under the weather?"

"I'm feeling fine!" Melissa insisted, although she'd already broken out in a sweat. "Three . . . four . . ." What was wrong with her? Melissa picked up the pace. "Five . . . six . . ."

She struggled through twelve reps, then hopped off the machine and forced a big smile. "What's next?" she asked, trying to sound chipper though her back and arms were aching.

"Bench press," Terry said. He checked his clipboard. "Let's see, McDormand, you're at one hundred ten pounds. Let's go for it."

"Doesn't Caitlin go first?" Melissa asked.

"What's the matter?" Caitlin asked. "You tired?"

Without another word, Melissa lay down on the red bench and slid along it until her shoulders were beneath the metal handles. Then she pushed up against the handles with all her strength. "One!" she counted. "Two!" But already her arms were so tired and she felt an overpowering urge to yawn. "Three! Four!"

Caitlin turned to Terry. "I don't think she looks so good."

"You wish, Bruneau!" Melissa said, though she knew in her heart that Caitlin was right. She'd never felt so weak at practice. Of course, she'd never stayed out till two in the morning, either. But one night out couldn't have done this to her!

By the time she'd gotten up to eight reps, Melissa knew she wouldn't be able to complete the series.

"Eight!" she cried, but she wasn't able to lift the weights all the way. She let them drop with a crash.

"Watch the equipment!" Terry said. "What's the matter, McDormand? You did this with no problem the other day."

Melissa slid off the bench, not knowing what to say. Should she lie and say she didn't feel well? Actually, that was half true. Or should she try to fake her way through the rest of the workout? From the way things were going so far, that probably wouldn't be possible.

"Let an expert show her," Caitlin said, moving the pin down a plate so that she'd be lifting one hundred twenty pounds. "She may have youth, but I have wisdom and experience. One . . ." she counted conversationally, seeming to press the weight above her head with no effort at all. "Two . . . Don't worry, McDormand. Your time will come. Just not as soon as you thought. Three . . ."

Terry shook his head. "Maybe you're right, Bruneau. I thought McDormand here was right on your tail, but maybe I was wrong." He checked his clipboard, then looked up again. "Where are my sprinters?" he asked loudly. There were scattered groans around the room. Without another word, Terry walked away.

Melissa sank down on the quadriceps bench, feeling mentally and physically drained. She had to bite her lip to keep the tears from coming to her eyes.

"Twelve!" Caitlin finished, letting the weights down. Then she sat up and faced Melissa. "Late night?" she asked.

Melissa was so surprised at Caitlin's perceptiveness that she couldn't even answer.

"Let me guess," Caitlin said. "That outdoorsy guy with the curly blond hair, right?"

Melissa nodded silently.

"I thought so," Caitlin said. "I recognized all the symptoms."

"Is Terry going to forget about me now?" Melissa asked in a small voice.

"Well, you didn't exactly impress him," Caitlin answered, "but if you clean up your act, he'll forget about it eventually."

"Clean up my act?"

"Do I have to lay it out for you?" Caitlin said. "I tried to warn you at the meet. You can't have a boyfriend *and* win the eight hundred. There just aren't enough hours in the day to do both. And it breaks up your concentration. For example, you're running heats at practice and worrying that you're going to be late for your date. Or you're out late with the guy and you can't enjoy yourself because you keep worrying you're not going to get enough sleep to be fresh for practice."

"You must be a mind reader," Melissa said glumly.

"Hardly," Caitlin said. "I've been there myself. I had a boyfriend freshman year—or let's say I *tried* to have one, but it just didn't work out. He was jealous of all the time I spent at practice, and Terry could tell I wasn't doing my best. Something had to give. Or some*one.*"

"You broke up?" Melissa asked.

Caitlin nodded. "It was the only way. If you want something badly enough, you have to make sacrifices."

"Bruneau!" Terry called from the opposite end of the room. "Get over here! I've got a freshman over here who thinks she can lift. Come put her in her place."

"Gotta go," Caitlin said.

"Thanks," Melissa said, leaning her elbows on her thighs and slumping forward. Caitlin was speaking truth—cold, hard truth—and Melissa was powerless to change it. Or was she? Maybe Caitlin hadn't organized her time efficiently enough. Maybe Caitlin had allowed herself to be distracted unnecessarily. Maybe a good relationship with a guy could actually improve an athlete's performance. Melissa had certainly run well when Brooks showed up at the first meet, and part of that had to be because he made her feel so good.

There *had* to be a way to make it work, and Melissa was going to find it. The first thing she was going to do was show her tired body who was boss.

Her powerful, focused brain was going to take charge and wouldn't take no for an answer.

Melissa got back onto the bench-press machine and placed her hands on the grips. The weights were still set at one hundred twenty pounds, but Melissa didn't care. If Caitlin could do it, she could. Taking a deep breath, Melissa closed her eyes and pushed. The weight lifted slowly, slowly, creaking upward as her arms shook. Then she let it down. That was one. She was going for twelve, and it didn't matter how long it took, or how much her chest muscles begged for mercy.

After bench press came biceps and triceps, abductors, adductors, and quadriceps, three sets of each, until Melissa's muscles were past begging. They were numb, practically paralyzed. Melissa looked at the clock on the wall. It was eight-thirty p.m., and she was all alone. She'd been so focused on her goal, and her pain, that she hadn't noticed when everyone else went home. Her stomach grumbled, but Melissa ignored it. She still had one more set of hamstrings before she would allow herself to even think about dinner.

Melissa lay face down on the bench and slipped her heels under the padded red cylinder. The weights were set at eighty pounds. Melissa gritted her teeth and clutched the handles as she bent her legs.

"One!" she shouted, though there was no one left to hear. She felt a twinge in her hamstring, but she had to keep going. If she just did nine more, she would have proven her mind was stronger than her body. "Two!" Melissa grunted. The twinge grew more painful.

Melissa let the weights down. She couldn't risk injuring her hamstring again or she could be out for months. Her mind and body both had failed.

Melissa did the only thing she could think of—the one thing she never did. She buried her face in her hands and she cried.

Seven

"More lemonade, Marielle?" the freshman asked politely. Marielle glanced up at the pretty girl leaning over her with an icy pitcher. The girl's straight brown hair was pulled back by a headband. She wore a powder pink cardigan sweater over a white silk blouse, a pink skirt, and black patent-leather pumps.

Marielle smiled sweetly at the freshman. She held out her glass for a refill.

As the freshman poured, careful not to spill a drop, Marielle delighted that this high-born girl, a San Francisco debutante whose father was chairman of a large insurance company, was catering to her.

Such were the privileges of being a junior in Beta Beta Beta. Though, of course, Marielle didn't want to push her advantage too far. Those lowly freshmen would be sophomores next year, and valuable contacts later on.

"Thank you," Marielle said as the girl moved on.

Marielle sat in one of the folding chairs set up at the back of Tri Beta's cozy living room, surrounded by her sorority sisters, who were listening raptly as their president, Courtney Conner, droned on. That girl did like to talk, Marielle observed sourly, though she was careful to keep a smile permanently plastered on her face.

". . . so let's turn now to the next item on our agenda," Courtney said. The willowy blond junior stood by the fireplace. Her beige velvet jacket perfectly complemented her creamy skin and hair. A hand-crocheted lace collar peeped out over the top of her jacket. Her slim beige skirt tastefully displayed her perfect body. Personally, Marielle found the outfit bland, although she knew every other girl in the sorority envied Courtney's expensive wardrobe.

"As some of you already know," Courtney began in her honey-smooth voice, "we will be making a rare exception in our rush procedure this year. Once in a very great while we come upon a girl so exceptional, so obviously Tri Beta material that we can't wait until the traditional fall rush to offer her a bid to join. This year, for the first time in Tri Beta history, we have found *three* such girls.

"I am proposing we invite these girls to a special tea in their honor so that we may get to know them better. In order for us to evaluate these girls properly, it is essential that every Tri Beta attend this tea and be prepared with thoughtful questions and smiles of welcome."

Smiles of welcome! Marielle groaned silently to herself. Courtney sounded like a Romper Room teacher. And the other girls were eating it up, nodding in agreement and hanging on Courtney's every word. Well, maybe they enjoyed being treated like children, but Marielle certainly didn't.

At that moment Courtney caught Marielle's eye and Marielle found her own head nodding and her lips spreading into a smile. As much as she resented Courtney, she wasn't willing to antagonize the president any further. Marielle had already been disciplined for past breaches of sorority rules. She couldn't afford to get in trouble again.

Courtney shifted her gaze to another girl and continued, "Now, I'd like to tell you a little bit about each of our guests so that you can plan what you'd like to ask them next week. First, there's KC

Angeletti. Some of you might remember her from fall rush. She was really, truly at the top of our list until an unfortunate incident prevented her from joining."

Several girls surreptitiously glanced at Marielle and smiled in a way that wasn't friendly. *Oh, please.* The whole house was acting as if it were Marielle's fault. Marielle had been with Mark Geisslinger at the Beanery one night during fall rush, speaking the complete, honest truth about that fat loser of a rushee, Lauren Turnbell-Smythe, when KC, who was working as a waitress, had spilled a milkshake all over Marielle. Next, KC had dropped out of sorority rush of her own accord. How could anybody blame Marielle?

Marielle pretended not to notice the looks.

Courtney blathered on. ". . . and she was the star attraction of the U of S Classic Calendar, which I'm sure most of you bought. Many say she's the most beautiful girl on campus. But did you know that she was also the brains behind the calendar? KC is a brilliant businesswoman with a bright future ahead of her."

Courtney had been going on about KC for five minutes. If she didn't stop soon, she wouldn't have time to talk about the other two girls. And what was so special about KC, anyway? Actually, *Kahia*

Cayanne. What kind of a name was that? A hippie name, like her hippie parents who sold bean sprouts or whatever it was. KC might try her best to hide it, but she was poor, dirt poor, with no background whatsoever.

What was wrong with Courtney that she didn't recognize trash when she saw it? Marielle had almost wanted to burst out laughing when KC offered to pay at the Beanery the day before. Marielle knew KC didn't have any money. And how many times did she plan to wear that green jacket with the acorn buttons? Didn't she have any other clothes? It made Marielle sick that people didn't see KC as clearly as she did.

The biggest joke, of course, was that KC had won freshman princess. Sure, she had good bone structure, but she was as far from being a princess as Marielle was from doing dishes. The night of Winter Formal, Marielle and Mark had been planning to help KC "slip" near a muddy construction pit so as to ruin her chances of winning. Before they could act, though, that girl with the weird clothes and spiky hair had beaten them to it and thrown KC into the pool.

That night, however, Marielle had had her brainstorm. She would *rescue* KC, act like her best friend, and set her up for an even bigger fall later on. It was a good thing she'd come up with that plan, or she never would have been able to stand it when Courtney ordered her to woo KC back into the sorority to make up for losing Lauren. (Nobody seemed to notice that Marielle had been right about that Tri Beta dropout after all.) It made Marielle sick to have to spend so much time with KC and feel invisible, while every cute guy within fifty miles drooled over her. It made her even sicker that Courtney fawned over KC, while she treated Marielle like dirt. But there was nothing she could do about it. If she didn't do what Courtney said, she'd get kicked out of Tri Beta, and that would have been worst of all.

The only thing that kept Marielle going was the knowledge that someday she was going to get back at KC without Courtney finding out. She didn't know how or when she was going to do it. She just knew that, one way or another, she would—and it would be great.

"That's beautiful, KC!" Faith exclaimed as KC held the red wool dress against herself and looked in the full-length mirror. The two friends stood in the back of the Vittorio Pugli boutique, surrounded by jewel-toned silk blouses, richly textured blazers, and butter-soft pants suspended from padded hangers. The store even *smelled* expensive.

KC sighed as she replaced the dress on the rack. "It doesn't matter how beautiful it is or how perfect it would look at the Tri Beta tea. I can't afford it."

"That's too bad," Faith said as KC fingered the sleeve of a bright green silk blouse with a shawl collar. "What about all the money you earned from the calendar? Isn't there any left?"

KC shook her head. "I blew it all on that dress for Winter Formal—which, I might add, I now use as a rag to shine my shoes, thanks to Winnie."

Faith winced. She'd asked KC to go shopping with her so she could tell KC about the party she was throwing for Winnie. Faith had planned to lead up to it gradually, first building up KC's sympathy by mentioning how distraught Winnie had been lately. But the way the conversation was heading, sympathy was the last thing KC would feel. Faith tried to steer the conversation away from Winnie.

"I wish I had some money to lend you," Faith said, "but I'm on a really tight budget. I mean, my parents give me money, but there's never anything left over."

"It was nice of you to offer," KC said, letting go of the blouse and heading for the front of the store.

"I guess I'll just have to recycle something from my closet. But I am so sick of all my clothes."

"Tell me about it," Faith said. "Why is it that no matter how many clothes you have, you still have nothing to wear?"

"One of the great unexplained laws of the universe," KC said. "And unless I can figure out how to break it, I might as well give up on becoming a Tri Beta."

KC held the door open as Faith headed out into the Springfield Mall. Polished wooden benches lined the mall, with potted ficus trees behind them. Ahead were the escalators leading down to the main level, where there were even more ficus trees and a very natural-looking waterfall.

"Is it really so important what you wear?"

"*Everything's* important," KC said. "They'll be scrutinizing me as if I were under a microscope, looking for the slightest imperfection."

Faith shuddered. "It sounds horrible."

"I know," KC said. "But it's worth it if I get in. It could make my entire future."

"No way," Faith said. "They're just a bunch of girls with headbands and cashmere cardigans."

"They're also the future Who's Who of America," KC said. "They come from the best families, they've had all the advantages, and they're the ones who'll be running the country twenty years from now. You'll see. And if I don't get to know them now, I'll never get the chance later on. Sororities are where you build your contacts for the future. I've got to get in, and I've got to look great, act great, and *be* great when I go to that tea. I can't afford to let anything go wrong."

As they neared the escalators, Faith slowed down.

"Where do you want to go next?" KC asked Faith.

This was as good a time as any for Faith to break the news to KC about Winnie's surprise party. "Let's sit down for a minute," Faith said.

"You tired?" KC asked.

"No, I want to talk to you."

"Uh-oh," KC said as they settled themselves on an empty bench. "Why do I have a feeling this is going to be another 'be nice to Winnie' conversation?"

"Because it is," Faith said seriously. "Just hear me out. Tuesday is Winnie's birthday, and I think it would be nice if we took the opportunity to show her how much we care about her. She's been really depressed lately, and I thought a surprise party would be just the thing to cheer her up."

"And what do you want *me* to do about it? You

know I still haven't forgiven her. And I can't turn off my anger just because it's her birthday."

"Why not?" Faith demanded. "I think that would be the perfect day for you two to make up. You can't spend the rest of your lives being mad at each other."

"Why not?" KC asked. "Maybe that was the end of our friendship, and now we're moving on. It happens, you know."

"But not to us!" Faith pleaded. "We've been friends since eighth grade. And Winnie's always been there when you needed her. Remember the time you were depressed because you didn't win first place at the Young Entrepreneurs' Convention and she climbed in your window in the middle of the night to cheer you up?"

"I haven't forgotten," KC said. "She sang me that crazy song."

"How did it go?" Faith tried to remember. " 'Cheer up, KC, don't you cry. I am here to tell you why. Don't worry yourself sick and skinny. You've got a friend and her name is Winnie.' "

KC groaned. "That was such a silly song."

"But it made you laugh, didn't it?"

"It didn't make my father laugh, when she climbed back out the window and fell the last few feet into the bushes. She made so much noise, he thought it was a burglar and called the police!"

"The point was, she tried," Faith said. "Which is more than you're doing right now. Look, it wouldn't be that hard. All you have to do is show up at the party and bring a nice present. Winnie will be so happy to see you, she'll do the rest. You just need to show her you're willing to try."

"First of all," KC said, "next Tuesday is the day of the Tri Beta tea. I can't be in two places at once."

"What time?" asked Faith.

"Four o'clock."

"Easy," Faith said. "We'll start the party at two-thirty. You can show up for a few minutes, make Winnie happy, then leave."

"I don't know," KC said. "That might be cutting it a little close. I need time to prepare. And second, I can't afford a nice present for Winnie. I can't afford *any* present. I just told you how broke I am."

"But aren't you still selling the calendar?" Faith asked. "It must bring in a little money."

"Very little," KC said. "It was more of a winter item. Now that we're a few months into the year, sales are almost zero. I can barely afford a cup of coffee."

Faith sighed and turned to watch the people

walking by. "Do it for me, then," she said almost under her breath.

KC found herself studying the sand-colored bricks beneath her feet. If she didn't want to be friends with Winnie anymore, she wasn't going to force herself just because that was what Faith wanted. On the other hand, how much trouble could it be to show up at a party?

"Maybe I could stop in for a quick hello."

Faith beamed. "Do you want to help me pick out decorations? There's a party store right downstairs."

"I guess so," KC said without much enthusiasm. The two girls got up and headed for the escalator.

At first, the young man walking toward them didn't look so much familiar as *comforting*. KC found his face completely unremarkable, forgettable even. His blondish hair wasn't cut in any particular style. His faded blue-jean jacket looked like millions of others. Then why did KC feel so happy as he approached?

As KC's heart flip-flopped, she realized what the answer was. The young man walking toward them was Peter Dvorsky, the photographer for the U of S Classic Calendar. The guy she'd planned to go to Winter Formal with before she dumped him for pretty boy Warren.

KC caught Peter's eye and smiled awkwardly. Faith saw Peter, too, and waved.

"What a coincidence!" Faith said as Peter approached. "What brings you here?"

"I'm looking for a new lens for my camera," Peter explained to Faith while looking out of the corner of his eye at KC. "What are you guys doing?"

"Well, KC was looking for something to wear to the Tri—" Faith began, but KC cut in.

"Just window shopping," she said firmly. She didn't want to let Peter know how concerned she was with her appearance at the sorority tea. She knew how he'd react. He'd smile that sardonic smile of his and make some joke about Barbie dolls. And much as she hated to admit it, she knew, deep down, that Peter was right.

That's what bothered her most about Peter: he made her look past the surface of things. It confused her. It made her doubt everything she was working for. And it made her feel guilty about all the people she was trying to outgrow, such as her parents and Winnie. It made her wonder if she really *was* growing, or just losing what little softness she had. Yes, Peter was definitely bad news. Then why couldn't she stop staring at him?

Peter stared back, started to say something, then stopped himself. "Well . . ." he started again.

"Um, yes," KC said. "We'd better be going. Nice seeing you again." KC grabbed Faith's arm and dragged her away.

"What was that all about?" Faith asked as they stepped on the escalator. "You were sort of rude to him, weren't you? I thought you liked him!"

"I don't know where you got that idea," KC said. "He's just an acquaintance, that's all. And I thought you said you wanted to look for decorations."

"I did, but he seems really nice. We certainly could have spent a few minutes—"

"I don't want to talk about him, okay?"

Eight

Brrring! Brrrring!

"Hello?" said Melissa. Even lifting the receiver made her arm ache. All her muscles ached, but she knew she was going to feel a lot worse when she woke up the next day.

"Where have you been?" Brooks asked accusingly. "I've been calling all evening."

"Practice," Melissa said tersely, throwing her knapsack on the bed and kicking off her worn-out sneakers. She'd just gotten back from the weight room, she hadn't even eaten yet, and now she had to contend with this.

"I had a nice time last night," Brooks said, his voice low and mellow. "A really nice time."

"*Yeah?*" Melissa said. "*Well, maybe you're here to have a nice time. Some of us have more important things to do.*"

"*What?*" Brooks asked, sounding confused. "*Are you okay?*"

"*No, I'm not okay,*" Melissa barked into the phone. "*I'm tired because I didn't get enough sleep, every muscle in my body hurts, my coach thinks I'm a failure, and it's all your fault.*"

"*My fault?*" Brooks demanded. "*What did I do?*"

"*You talked me into going out on a weeknight when you knew full well I couldn't afford the time. If you really cared about me, you would have encouraged me to study.*"

"*Melissa! It was just one night!*"

"*I know. But maybe one night was too much.*"

The previous night's conversation repeated itself over and over in Melissa's mind as she stretched by the side of the red oval track. Practice was about to start and despite her efforts to undo the damage she'd done to her body in the weight room, every muscle was stiff and sore. But that was nothing compared to the pain she felt inside. She felt guilty about the way she'd suddenly treated Brooks. She shouldn't have been so short. But she was still furious with him and furious with herself for letting go like that.

And she had to face Terry again. Talk about coming from behind. She was behind the eight ball as far as her coach was concerned, and she'd have to make up a lot of ground before he'd respect her again.

There was a sharp toot from Terry's whistle. "Eight hundred meters!" he called.

Melissa took her mark and waited, as half a dozen others took theirs on the staggered starting lines. She glanced toward the center of the oval, where long jumpers were taking practice runs, three long strides then a flying leap over a long sand pit. Behind them, high jumpers ran toward a high bar, then threw themselves over it. Everyone else seemed so relaxed, so confident, so business-as-usual, and Melissa felt as if her whole future depended on this one practice.

Then she noticed Brooks leaning against the fence in the exact same position he'd been in before her first meet. He caught her eye, waved, and offered a tentative smile.

The feeling that came over Melissa then was very different from what she'd felt when she'd seen him at the meet. A knot formed and tightened in her stomach. A thin line of pain shot through her head and turned into a thumping, throbbing ache. Brooks was suddenly a living reminder of all the people and forces that were pulling on her from every direction.

"Runners, take your marks!" Terry shouted.

Melissa placed her left foot in front of her right and took a deep breath. It was bad enough she wasn't running her best and that she'd lost Terry's respect the day before, but with Brooks watching, there was no way—

A blast from Terry's whistle interrupted Melissa's thoughts, and her legs started moving. *At least my legs remember what to do,* Melissa thought ruefully as she headed down the first straightaway. The rest of her had forgotten the drill. She hadn't cleared her mind or visualized winning or any of the things she usually did even in practice. And it was a little late to start because she was coming around the first curve, her legs felt like lead, and there went Caitlin, taking the lead as usual.

Well, maybe it was time for a change of plan. Why should Caitlin always start out in front? Ignoring her pounding head and upset stomach, Melissa pumped her legs and arms, trying to catch up. Caitlin didn't have much of a kick. If Melissa could just keep pace with her, then pour on a little extra at the end . . .

Melissa's heart felt as if it would burst from her chest as she tried to overtake Caitlin on the second straightaway. She shortened the distance between them, but just as she was about to make her move, Jamie Oscarson appeared from nowhere and placed herself between Melissa and Caitlin. Melissa poured on more speed, but then Marilyn Unruh was at her left shoulder, trying to pass from the inside.

As Terry blew the whistle, signaling the last lap, Marilyn pulled ahead. Melissa was in fourth place, Caitlin was disappearing in the distance, and Mathilda Levin was quickly moving up from fifth. Melissa tried desperately to give more, but she had nothing left. Not only had she used up her kick, but her headache had gotten so bad that she wasn't sure if she'd even be able to finish the race!

Mathilda passed Melissa on the backstretch, quickly followed by Elaine Greenberg. Melissa was in last place! By the time she rounded the last corner, Caitlin had already crossed the finish line, followed by Marilyn and Jamie. The best Melissa could do was not slow down. She had to at least act as if she hadn't given up completely, but she was sucking wind so hard she thought she was going to collapse.

Melissa stumbled over the finish line, gasping for breath. Her legs felt as though they were on fire.

Terry was waiting for her, holding up one of his stopwatches, a scowl on his face. "What kind of a race was that?" he demanded as Melissa passed him.

Melissa made a U-turn and ran back to Terry, her face red and flushed. "A bad one," she admitted guiltily.

"You see these numbers?" Terry asked, holding the stopwatch near her eyes. "You want to read that for me?"

Though Melissa knew she'd run poorly, she was still amazed to see how awful the truth really was. Terry's watch said two minutes seven seconds. She'd run the eight hundred fifteen seconds slower than she had at the meet.

"What happened to your kick?" Terry yelled. "What were you trying to do out there? Change the rules? You don't have the speed to lead the whole race. By trying to lead, you lost your kick. No wonder you came in last!"

Melissa wished she could run away—from the track, from school, from Springfield altogether—only she didn't even have the energy. All she could do was stand there and try not to cry. Out of the corner of her eye, Melissa noticed that Brooks had wandered over and was listening to every horrible word. Caitlin, too, had casually trotted toward Terry as if she were just cooling down, but Melissa knew she was listening, too. It had to be the most humiliating moment of her track career, if not her entire life, and the last thing she needed was witnesses.

"Stick with the kick, McDormand," Terry warned, "or you might not get to start at the next meet." Terry blew his whistle, then called out to the rest of the runners. "Okay!" he shouted. "Five-minute water break, then the four hundred."

As Terry walked toward the center of the oval to oversee the long jumpers, Caitlin placed a hand on Melissa's shoulder. As Melissa looked up, Caitlin smiled sympathetically, glanced over at Brooks, who hovered nearby, then looked back at Melissa. "I hate to say I told you so," she said, "but I wasn't kidding when I said you can't have it all."

"I didn't want to believe you," Melissa whispered. "I thought I could figure out a way to make it work."

"If you ever do," Caitlin said, "let me know. I'm going to get some water."

As Caitlin trotted away, Melissa looked over in Brooks's direction. He was looking down at the ground, his hands in his pockets, trying to act as if he hadn't heard. But if it hadn't been for him, she would have been rested the day before when she went to the weight room and she wouldn't have embarrassed herself. Then she wouldn't have over-done it after everyone had gone home, and she would have run better that day, especially if he hadn't shown up to distract her. Caitlin had been right. Brooks was standing in the way of everything she was trying to hold on to—her track scholarship, her grades, and her place at U of S!

Melissa glared at Brooks as he approached.

"How's it going?" he asked casually, though his eyes showed concern.

"Not too great," Melissa said. Then she added in a whisper, "Thanks to you."

"What did *I* do?" Brooks asked, his eyebrows raised in surprise. "I was just trying to show you a little support."

"With support like that, I might as well quit the team." Melissa sighed.

"What are you saying?" Brooks demanded.

"I'm saying please don't hover over me like I need protection. I'm not Faith. Is that clear enough for you?"

"As a matter of fact, it's not," Brooks said. "I'd like you to explain to me how we could have had such a great time the other night, then you cut me off on the phone last night and talk to me today as if I'm some sort of creep. All I did was try to show you how much I care."

"You don't care about me," Melissa snarled. "You care so much that you don't notice you could cost me my place on the team and my scholarship. That's not caring."

"That's not true—" Brooks began, but Melissa interrupted him.

"Did it ever occur to you that every second I spend with you is a second less devoted to my work and to track practice? I thought I could make it work, Brooks, I really did, but I just don't have the time to have a boyfriend and be a top runner, too."

Melissa turned to walk away, but Brooks grabbed her arm. "So that's it?" he demanded, his eyes flashing with hurt and anger. *"You* decide it's over and that makes it over? Don't I have anything to say about this?"

"I'm at practice, in case you hadn't noticed," Melissa said, her insides clamping shut.

"So how about somewhere else?" Brooks suggested. "Later tonight. We could meet for a cup of coffee and talk about it."

"Later tonight I will be finishing all the reading I didn't get to the last two nights," Melissa said. Again she tried to leave, but Brooks would not let go of her arm.

"You promised me you wouldn't do this," he pleaded. "You promised you wouldn't string me along and then dump me without warning. You said you wouldn't play games."

"I'm not playing games," Melissa said.

"Then tell me exactly where we stand," Brooks demanded. "Are we still seeing each other or not? Are we on or off?"

"We're off!" Melissa blurted, wrenching her arm out of his grasp and running away as fast as her exhausted legs would allow.

Nine

....

KC turned up her nose when she saw Lauren's dinner tray. "Tofu with mixed vegetables?" she sniffed as Lauren took a seat beside her in the dining commons. "Did you have to dig up somebody's garden to get that?"

Faith, sitting on the opposite side of the table from KC, laughed. "You're the last person I'd expect to make fun of a meal like that. Isn't that one of the most popular dishes at your parents' restaurant?"

"It may be," KC said, "but I'm proud to say I've never tasted it. The whole concept of bean curd just turns my stomach. It's so slippery and squishy."

"And it's my dinner," Lauren said calmly, "so I'd appreciate your refraining from such a vivid and unflattering description of it. It happens to be delicious, not to mention low in calories. I'm trying to eat more carefully." Lauren removed her green satin bomber jacket and hung it on the back of her chair. She wore an oversized white shirt with a patchwork vest and olive army pants.

"Well, I hope you're not planning to diet at Winnie's party," Faith said. "I'm ordering a six-foot sandwich from Super Hero." She pulled a folded piece of paper out of the pocket of her jeans. "I've got my list for the party right here."

"I might allow myself a bite," Lauren said.

"Well, I'm sure Dash will eat a foot or so," Faith said. "You're inviting him, aren't you?"

"I don't know." Lauren poked at the bean curd and vegetables with her fork, stirring them around on her plate.

"Why not?" Faith asked. "Is something wrong?"

Lauren shrugged and speared a piece of broccoli, which she held up to her nose and examined as if she'd never seen anything like it before.

"No!" KC exclaimed, sensing Lauren's distress. "You and Dash are so great together, I can't believe it's anything serious."

"He lied to me!" Lauren exclaimed. While Faith

and KC stared in surprise, Lauren continued. "Well, not lied exactly, but withheld important information."

"What kind of information?" asked KC. "About some article you're working on?"

"No, much worse," Lauren said. "On Saturday his family is meeting him for dinner at this restaurant in town, and he never even mentioned it."

"How do you know they're coming if he never mentioned it?" asked KC.

Lauren blushed again. "I happened to see a letter he got from his parents," she began.

"Lauren!" Faith said in mock dismay.

Lauren shrugged. "I saw the letter on his desk at the *Journal*. But the thing that bothers me the most is, when I confronted him with it, he really *did* lie. He said they'd already been here. That obviously means he doesn't want them to meet me, and I have to ask myself why."

"Maybe it has nothing to do with you," Faith suggested. "Maybe they're only here for a quick visit and there's no time to include you."

"Thank you for looking on the bright side," Lauren said, "but I already figured out the real reason. Dash is ashamed to introduce his family to a society snob like me. But he's wrong! If I could just meet them, I could prove to them that I'm not stuck-up and spoiled and selfish. I'm sure they'd like me if they gave me a chance, but now they never will because Dash is determined to keep us apart."

"Lauren," KC said, "I'd give anything to have your problems."

"I don't understand," Lauren said.

"Think about it," KC said. "Right now you're worried that Dash's parents won't like you because you're too rich. Remember what happened to me when I met Steven Garth's father? It was exactly the opposite. Steven's family is really rich, and I'm poor, and if Steven hadn't treated me like the pauper I am, I might still be going out with him right now."

"Oh," Lauren said thoughtfully. "I never looked at it that way."

"And you have an even bigger problem that I'd give my future bank account for," KC continued. "Your mother cut you off because you refused to be a Tri Beta. One of my biggest goals in life right now is to get *into* the Tri Betas. I think you and I were born into the wrong families."

"My mother would love you," Lauren admitted.

"And my parents would adore you," KC said. "You have all the values they haven't been able to instill in me—you're working for the good of humanity, you're not materialistic, and you even like vegetables."

"Maybe you guys should trade places." Faith giggled. "The princess and the pauperette."

"Except *she's* the princess," Lauren said. "Freshman princess, anyway."

"Yeah, but you've got the wardrobe, even if you never wear it anymore," KC said. "I wish I had even half of what you have in your closet. I feel like such a jerk every time the Tri Betas see me in this same green jacket. They'll probably laugh at me when they see it again at the Tri Beta tea."

"Why don't you borrow something of mine?" Lauren asked. "I know you're a lot thinner than I am, so you'd probably swim in my clothes, but I might have something else you could borrow. Accessories, maybe, or some jewelry. Come on," she said, getting up from the table, "let's go raid my closet."

"Are you sure?" KC asked.

"Positive," Lauren said with a smile. She turned to Faith. "Are you going back to the room?"

Faith shook her head. "You guys have fun. I want to sit here and go over plans for Winnie's birthday. You're both coming, right?"

KC stood abruptly and picked up her tray.

"Ready when you are, Lauren," she said brightly. "See you later, Faith."

"Oh, I just don't know!" KC wailed as she lay on Faith's bed a few minutes later. "All your things are beautiful, Lauren, but I'm so afraid of making the wrong decision. They're going to be watching everything I say and do."

"Like vultures," Lauren agreed. "And they'll be ready to pick you apart, that's for sure."

KC groaned. "Oh, why couldn't I have been a legacy, just like you? Then I wouldn't have to go through all this." Suddenly KC laughed.

"What's so funny?" Lauren asked as she pulled a few more scarves from the rack in her closet and laid them out on her bed.

"I was just imagining my mother in a sorority," KC said. "I've seen pictures of her from college. She had this long, messy braid, and faded bell-bottom jeans with rips in them. Not exactly Tri Beta material."

Lauren laughed, too. "No, but she sounds really neat. So none of this stuff is right?" She indicated the huge pile of shoes, scarves, and belts on her bed.

"They're all beautiful," KC moaned. "I just can't make up my mind."

"How about these?" Lauren said, opening her jewelry box and pulling out a strand of pearls. "They go with anything, and no sorority sister should be seen without them."

KC sat up and took the pearls from Lauren's outstretched hand. "They're gorgeous," she breathed, holding them up to the light. "Look, they even have pink highlights. I love them." She looked up hopefully at Lauren.

"Take them," Lauren said. "You can give them back after they accept you, which I'm sure they will. KC, you were *born* to be a Tri Beta, no matter who your parents are."

KC smiled gratefully. "I guess it's not so much where you come from as where you're going, right? I mean, ultimately we have to make our own decisions about what we want to do with our lives. It's not up to our parents."

"That's right!" Lauren said softly, her violet eyes unfocused.

"What are you thinking about?" KC said.

"I'm thinking about what you just said," Lauren said. "About how it's up to us. I'm free to act however I want, especially now that my parents have left me on my own. And I can make my own decisions about what's important."

"I have a feeling you're talking about Dash," KC said with a grin.

"You've got that right," Lauren said. "I'm in love with him. I can't hide from his family. If they don't like me, that's their decision, but they've got to meet me first."

"But how are you going to arrange that?" KC asked. "You can't just walk into the restaurant where they're having dinner and say, 'Hi, I'm Lauren.'"

Lauren's eyes started to gleam. Then she grabbed KC and planted a kiss on her cheek.

"What?" KC asked with some alarm. "What did I say?"

"That's it!" Lauren exclaimed. "You've just solved my problem."

"No." KC clutched the side of Faith's bed in disbelief. "You wouldn't really crash their dinner?"

"Wouldn't I?" Lauren asked defiantly. "What do I have to lose? If I never meet them, I'll never know the truth, and if I can't face the truth, there's no point going on with Dash."

"I can't believe you're really going to do it," KC said.

"Try and stop me!" Lauren said, with a new edge to her voice.

* * *

Faith smiled as she went over the guest list for Winnie's party. Almost thirty people. Seeing how many people cared about her should make Winnie feel better.

Faith went to the next item on her master list: food. Besides the six-foot hero, she'd purchased several large bottles of soda, munchies, and candy, which now waited in a box under her bed. Item three, decorations, was also taken care of. Crepe-paper streamers and a big, colorful Happy Birthday sign sat in a paper bag at the bottom of her closet. Now all she had to do was figure out how to surprise Winnie.

Faith looked up from her list and spotted a familiar figure dumping a tray at the kitchen window. Even from a distance, it was hard to miss those golden curls and the familiar down vest. It was Brooks. But there was something different about him. His usual bouncing, athletic stride had slowed, and he had big circles under his eyes, as if he hadn't slept. As Brooks came even closer, she noticed that he hadn't shaved and his expression was gloomy.

Faith's first impulse was to flag him down and ask what was wrong, but she stopped herself. Maybe she didn't have the right to do that anymore. They weren't boyfriend and girlfriend, and they weren't really friends yet. But at least she could say hi.

Faith waved shyly. "Brooks!" she called.

Brooks didn't seem to hear her.

"Brooks!" she called louder. "Over here!"

This time Brooks looked up, only he looked at her as if she were a stranger. Was it because he was upset, or had they really come to that? Two strangers who used to be intimate.

"Hi," Brooks said morosely, threading his way through the tables toward her.

Faith decided to take a chance. If Brooks didn't want to answer, he didn't have to. "Is something wrong?" she asked.

"Oh . . ." Brooks shrugged. "I'm okay. Just a little tired."

Faith didn't want to force the issue, so she pretended to believe him. "I guess the Honors College is a lot harder than high school," she said, "especially with all your other activities, like intramural soccer. No wonder you're tired."

"It's not so bad," Brooks said. "I'm sure lots of other students carry heavier loads than I do. It's not like I'm on a varsity team or anything." Brooks pulled back a chair and sat on it sideways. "So, how are things going with you?"

"Pretty busy," Faith said. "At least, I will be once

I start my next theater project. Only I guess you couldn't call it a theater project, exactly. It's more like a film project."

Brooks's mood lifted a little as his face brightened with interest. "Film?" he asked. "Are you making a movie?"

"Not exactly," Faith said, "but I'll be working on one. I've been recommended to be an intern when this film company comes to the university. The good news is that it's a real Hollywood movie with a real director and real stars and everything. The bad news is that I'm just going to be a gofer. I'll probably be sharpening the producers' pencils."

"But who knows where it could lead?" Brooks pointed out. "You could do such a good job that they'll hire you when you get out of school, or maybe the director will discover you and offer you a role in his next movie."

"Let's not get carried away," Faith said, "but I'll be thrilled even if sharpening pencils is all I ever do."

"That's great, Faith," Brooks said with a genuine smile. "You've worked really hard to get this far, and now you're starting to get some of the rewards."

"It *is* nice," Faith agreed.

"Are those notes for the movie project?" Brooks

asked, pointing to the piece of paper in front of Faith.

Faith laughed. "No! That's off in the future. Actually this is my list of things to do for a surprise party I'm throwing for Winnie. Her birthday's next Tuesday."

"That's really nice of you," Brooks said.

"Do you want to come?" Faith asked. "I mean, you've known her as long as KC or I have, and I'm sure she'd be happy to see you. There's going to be a six-foot hero and lots of other food."

"You don't have to sell me," Brooks said. "I'd love to come. Can I help with anything?"

"Actually . . ." Faith was starting to get an idea. "We need someone to get Winnie to the party without her knowing what's going on."

"What time does it start?" Brooks asked.

"Two-thirty."

Brooks grew thoughtful for a moment. Then he said, "I haven't seen Winnie for a while. I could call her and ask her if she wants to go running with me. Of course, that would mean we'd be all sweaty for the party."

"How about a light jog?" Faith suggested. "You could take her past my dorm and act like you want to stop by my room and say hello. That will take you right past the common room, where we'll be all set up for the party."

"Gotcha!" Brooks said. "I'll try to throw something at the window to let you know we're on our way up."

"Good idea," Faith said.

They sat there for a moment smiling at each other, not in a romantic way but just like two good friends who felt comfortable with each other. Maybe they *had* reached the point where they could be friends without any lingering bitterness or resentment. Of course Faith still felt a touch of jealousy that he was involved with someone else, but maybe that would disappear, too, in time. She wondered how Brooks's relationship with Melissa was going, but she didn't feel she could ask him yet.

"Well," Brooks said, slowly rising from his chair, "I guess I'd better hit the books." He sighed.

"You sure you're okay?" Faith asked. "Is there anything you'd like to talk about?"

"Nah," Brooks said. "I've just got a lot of studying to do tonight. I'll call Winnie tomorrow and set the whole thing up."

"Thanks," Faith said.

Faith sat at her table, thinking about Brooks, after he'd gone. No matter how much he denied it, there was definitely something bothering him. She'd known him too long to be fooled by his words. His face and body said otherwise.

Ten

This is war! Lauren thought as she studied her reflection in the full-length mirror on the back of her closet door. She had her battle strategy all mapped out. She was armed with the address of Moreno's, the restaurant where Dash was meeting his parents for dinner.

The girl who stared back at Lauren from the mirror wore a drab beige dress bought at a second-hand clothing store especially for the occasion. It was perfect. It was shabby enough so no one would guess how rich her parents were, but it wasn't torn or ripped. That would be too obvious.

Lauren was ready. Now all she had to do was find

the restaurant. She hoped it wasn't in too dangerous a part of town. Dash's parents probably couldn't afford very much, though, so Lauren was prepared for the worst. She'd put aside some money from her job at the Springfield Mountain Inn, so she could take a taxi to and from the restaurant. That way, at least, she wouldn't have to walk dirty, deserted streets alone.

Throwing her green satin bomber jacket over her dress, Lauren grabbed her money and keys and left her room. The sound of a violin warming up down the hall and the smell of turpentine brought a lump to her throat. What if, despite all her precautions, something bad happened to her on the streets outside the restaurant and she never made it back to her dorm? Lauren tried to tell herself how silly she was for worrying, but she left Coleridge Hall with a growing sense of doom.

When Lauren opened the front door of the dorm, she saw the cab she'd called waiting right outside. Lauren gave the driver the address and settled back in her seat. She tried to calm her pounding heart as they drove away from campus. The mountains and trees surrounded them on all sides, as if they were at the bottom of a huge bowl. In all this natural beauty, it was hard to imagine a dirty, squalid restaurant and dingy streets.

The driver turned into The Strand, Springfield's fancy section with designer boutiques and expensive restaurants. Lauren sighed as she looked out the window. Fashionably dressed men and women were strolling up and down the broad sidewalks, dining at outdoor cafés, and looking in shop windows. Very soon, the taxi would leave all that as it headed for the older, run-down section of town.

The taxi pulled over to the curb and the driver turned off the meter.

"Three fifty," he said, turning around.

Lauren looked at him in surprise. "We can't be there yet," she said. "Did you check the address?"

The driver pointed out the window. A pearl gray awning on gleaming brass poles extended along the sidewalk to the curb. Written on the awning in graceful, curving script was the word *Moreno's*. A doorman, resplendent in a pearl gray uniform that matched the awning, marched toward the taxi and opened the door.

"Good evening, miss," he said, tipping his hat.

"Is there another Moreno's in Springfield?" Lauren asked the doorman.

"No, miss," he said politely. "This is the only one in town."

Still confused, Lauren paid the driver and allowed the doorman to help her out of the cab. As the doorman closed the car door, Lauren wandered towards the heavy brass-and-glass doors of the restaurant. Maybe she had made a mistake after all. The letter *had* been in Spanish. Maybe Dash's mother had written about friends of theirs named Moreno. Lauren was tempted to run back to the cab and get a ride back to campus, but as long as she was there, she decided to check inside, just to make sure.

The doorman, already at the door, held it open for Lauren as she passed into the vestibule. A crystal vase filled with exotic flowers stood on an antique table beneath a carved mirror. Lauren walked a few steps farther and came to a mahogany podium. Behind it stood a handsome middle-aged man wearing a tuxedo.

"Good evening," said the maître d', discreetly ignoring her bomber jacket and drab dress. "Do you have a reservation?"

"I'm, um, not sure," Lauren admitted. "I'm supposed to be meeting the Ramirez family. I believe they have a seven-thirty reservation, though I could have gotten the date wrong."

"Oh, no," the maître d' said, checking an open leather-bound volume on the podium. "I have them down for seven-thirty, and I believe they've already arrived. Would you like to check your . . . jacket?"

Lauren fingered her jacket nervously. "No, thank you," she said. "I'm not sure how long I'll be staying."

"Very good," the maître d' said. "Cosette will escort you to your table."

There had to be some mistake, Lauren thought. Dash's family could never afford to eat in this restaurant!

A pretty young woman with short blond hair and bright red lipstick beckoned Lauren. Lauren followed the woman into a large, elegant dining room. Each table was covered with a pearl gray linen cloth and had a tasteful arrangement of flowers and candles in the middle. Tuxedoed waiters and busboys hovered nearby, serving, removing empty plates, or pushing a dessert cart laden with cakes, mousses, and pies. The only sounds were the occasional clinking of silverware and the low hum of conversation.

Cosette led Lauren across the room, stopping before a large picture window facing the front of the restaurant. "Here is your party," she said, smiling and indicating a large round table.

All Lauren could do was gape. Though one of the faces was familiar, she still couldn't believe what she saw. Dash, clean-shaven for once and wearing an expensive-looking gray suit, his hair pulled back, sat on one of the silk-upholstered chairs. Next to him was an attractive young woman with curly dark hair that reached her shoulders. She wore a fitted black jacket with beige polka dots and chunky gold earrings with black onyx stones.

Across from Dash and the young woman sat a distinguished-looking older man with a full head of gray hair and a mustache. He wore a navy pin-striped suit, a white oxford button-down shirt, and a red paisley tie. Beside him sat an exquisitely beautiful woman in a flowing red silk dress with a white silk blazer. Her hair was also dark and curly, though it was laced with strands of white.

They all stared at Lauren pleasantly.

"And who do we have here?" asked the older man. His voice had the same lilting accent as Dash's, though it was deeper and carried more authority. Could he really be Dash's father?

"Hi, Dash," Lauren said meekly.

"Is this a friend of yours?" asked the older woman, turning her beautiful black eyes towards Dash. "Why don't you invite her to join us?" Her voice, too, was slightly accented.

Dash half rose from his chair, his face beet red. He stared at Lauren as if she were a ghost. "Hi,

Lauren," he said, just as meekly, though Lauren detected a flash of anger in his eyes.

"Is this your family?" Lauren asked, still unable to believe what she saw.

Dash nodded.

"Well, get your friend a chair!" exclaimed Mrs. Ramirez.

Dash waved his hand, and a waiter instantly appeared. "We'd like another chair, please," Dash said, his voice just above a whisper.

The waiter vanished and reappeared mere seconds later. "Madame," he said as he seated Lauren.

Lauren didn't know what to say. She just stared at the fine gray tablecloth and shining silverware. Then she scanned the faces surrounding her. They still seemed amused, except for Dash's.

"I'm awfully sorry to interrupt your dinner," she apologized.

"Nonsense!" said Mr. Ramirez. "We haven't even ordered yet. Besides, we're very happy to meet one of Dash's friends. From the way he talks, you'd think he does nothing but study."

"Oh, he does a lot more than that," Lauren said. "I mean, he studies, don't get me wrong, but he's very active on campus." Lauren glanced at Dash to see how he was reacting to this, but he was stone-cold silent. She was obviously on her own. "I'm Lauren Turnbell-Smythe, by the way."

Mr. Ramirez rose in his chair and gave a little bow.

Mrs. Ramirez leaned forward eagerly. "So tell me about yourself," she asked Lauren. "Do you have any classes with Dash?"

"No," Lauren admitted, "but we've written some articles together for the campus paper."

"Following in my footsteps," said Mr. Ramirez proudly. "I thought I was going to be a professional journalist while I was in college. Almost did it, too, until I realized there wasn't much money in it."

Mrs. Ramirez poked her husband playfully. "Oh, don't be so crass."

Mr. Ramirez smiled broadly, and Lauren recognized Dash in him.

"What do you do, Mr. Ramirez?" she asked respectfully.

"I work for a bank," he said.

Anna rolled her eyes. "He always says that," she said. "He's actually the *president* of a bank."

Lauren was shocked. All Dash had said was that his father had a steady job, nothing worth going into. Modesty was one thing, but that was almost an out-and-out lie. President of a bank? That meant

Dash's family had money. Dash had always acted as if his family were poor. That meant his streetwise attitude was all an act!

Lauren shot an accusing look at Dash. He looked at her just as angrily, but she wasn't afraid anymore of what he might think. She just wanted to know how else he had tried to deceive her.

"And you, Mrs. Ramirez?" she asked, remembering Dash had said his mother did paperwork in a hospital. "Do you work?"

"Oh yes," Mrs. Ramirez said. "After all those years getting my MBA, I wasn't about to waste it sitting around getting my nails done. I'm chief administrator of Wildwood Hospital."

Lauren couldn't wait to find out what Dash had really meant when he said his sister was involved with the law. "Tell me about you, Anna," she said sweetly.

"I'm in my first year of law school at Columbia," Anna said. "It's really brutal, too. I call Dash all the time to tell him how much trouble I'm having."

Lauren was fuming inside. Dash had just about implied his sister was a felon when she was actually in the Ivy League! No matter how angry Dash might be that Lauren had barged in, Lauren knew she was a whole lot angrier.

"Anna's not having trouble," her mother corrected her. "She got three A's and one B last semester."

"That's what I'm talking about," Anna said. "I never got a B before I got to law school. And I'm certainly not going to get another one."

Mr. Ramirez beamed proudly. "That's my girl!"

A waiter approached with his pad. "Would you like to hear the specials?" he asked.

"Oh yes, please," said Mrs. Ramirez. She turned to Lauren. "Please say you'll join us for dinner."

"I believe Lauren said she has other plans," Dash said, looking at Lauren with daggers in his eyes.

"Oh, can't you break them?" Anna asked, squeezing Lauren's arm. "We definitely approve of Dash's girlfriend." She pinched Dash's cheek. "I can't believe it! My little brother's a grown-up college man! I remember pushing him around in my doll carriage! He was so cute and roly-poly!"

Dash shot his sister a withering look. "I may be younger than you," he warned, "but I'm a lot bigger than you are."

"I'm so scared," Anna said sarcastically, sticking out her tongue.

Mrs. Ramirez clucked her tongue at them disapprovingly. "When will you two grow up? You're adults now and you *still* don't know how to behave in a restaurant. So, Lauren, are you sure you can't stay?"

Lauren took one look at Dash and knew immediately what her answer would be. "Thank you anyway," she said, "but I really can't. I just wanted to stop by and say hello."

"Oh." Anna looked disappointed.

Lauren rose to leave. "It was a pleasure meeting all of you," she said. "Dash has told me *so* much about you."

Dash rose also. "I'll walk you out," he said. Taking Lauren's arm, he half led, half dragged her from the restaurant.

For a moment they just stood on the sidewalk outside the restaurant, glaring at each other. Then they both started yelling at once.

"You have some nerve barging in on my family!" Dash screamed.

"Dash Ramirez, you are the biggest liar on the face of the earth!" Lauren shouted back, not even listening to him. She was almost surprised by the sound of her own voice.

"I never lied to you," Dash said. "Everything I said about my family was true."

"It's what you *didn't* say that makes me so mad,"

Lauren said. "You just about implied you were a disadvantaged youth struggling to get by."

"I was just joking around!" Dash protested. "I never said my family was poor."

"You sure acted as if they were," Lauren said, "with your bandanna and your streetwise attitude. The only street you're from is Easy Street! I can't believe all the grief you gave me because my parents have money. You and all your talk about 'bourgeois hypocrisy'—*you're* the biggest hypocrite I've ever met in my entire life!"

"And you have the worst manners!" Dash yelled back. "If I'd wanted to invite you to dinner, I would have. You had no right to read my mail and just appear at the restaurant."

"And why *didn't* you invite me, I'd like to know?" Lauren shot back. "You want to know what I think? I think you were afraid I'd find out the truth about your family and blow your cover. You were afraid that once word got around campus that your family was well off, no one would take you seriously as Dash Ramirez the Avenger, Righter of Social Wrongs, Defender of the Underclass."

"Interesting theory," Dash said. "Did it ever occur to you that there might have been a simpler explanation? Like maybe I just didn't want you to come?"

"Oh yeah? Well, the only reason I showed up was to prove to myself what a jerk you really are!" Lauren stormed off down the sidewalk.

"Nice outfit!" Dash screamed after her.

Eleven

....

"**H**appy birthday to you, Happy birthday to you . . ." Faith sang to herself, keeping time to the beat of the song with her feet as she strode rapidly to KC's dorm.

Winnie's birthday had finally arrived and in a few hours Faith hoped to give her the present that would mean the most—KC. No matter how hard Faith had tried to pin KC down, KC had never promised she would come to Winnie's party. But Faith was determined to get that promise from KC, or else.

"*Happy birthday, dear Winnie . . .*"

Faith hopped up the steps of the glassed-in porch outside Langston House and headed inside. Unlike the plain brick 1950s dorm where Faith lived, Langston House had the charm and detail of the Victorian era. An all-girls study dorm, it was peaceful and quiet. It even had lace curtains in the windows.

"Happy birthday to you."

Faith rapped on KC's door.

"Who is it?" came the nervous voice from inside. Could that really be KC? She didn't sound like her cool, normal self.

"It's Faith," Faith announced.

"Are you alone?"

"Yes."

The door opened a crack. "Come in quickly," KC said, "and lock the door behind you."

Curious about KC's strange behavior, Faith obeyed. When she turned around, she quickly realized why KC hadn't wanted anyone to see her. KC was a mess. Her hair stood out from her head in a frizzy mess. She wore no makeup and had nothing on but a baggy man's undershirt and a pair of panties. Every other piece of clothing she owned was scattered all over the room.

"Whoa!" Faith exclaimed. "If those Tri Betas could see you now!"

"Don't even think of it," KC said. "The tea is in

less than three hours and I still have nothing to wear."

"You'll figure out something," Faith said. "By the time you get to Winnie's party, I'm sure you'll look lovely."

Ignoring Faith, KC stepped over the skirts and blouses and stared at her face in the mirror over her dresser. "This is a disaster!" she cried. "Would you look at this? I figured I'd try something different with my hair, you know, smooth it down, maybe pull it back with a headband, but all I got was frizz! I never should have used a hairbrush in my hair. I should have just let it dry naturally like I usually do."

"So wet it again," Faith said.

KC leaned in closer toward the mirror. "Oh no! It's just one thing after another. Is that a pimple?" She turned to face Faith. "How noticeable is it?"

"It's microscopic," Faith said. "Now please, KC, will you listen to me for one minute? Then I'll leave so you can get ready."

"Fine, fine," KC said, "but a minute is really all I have to spare." She sat down in her desk chair, then immediately got up again. "I can't sit down," she said. "I'm too jumpy. But go ahead, I'm listening."

"Okay," Faith said, trying to calm KC with the

tone of her voice. "I just wanted to go over the details of Winnie's party with you."

"Winnie's party!" KC exclaimed. "I forgot all about it. I didn't even buy her a present. You know, with this tea, there was so much on my mind."

It was worse than Faith had thought. But whether KC really had forgotten or was snubbing Winnie on purpose, Faith didn't care. The present wasn't even that important—just as long as KC showed up.

"I'll tell you what," Faith said, "you can sign your name on my card. We'll say my present was from both of us."

"What did you get her?" KC asked.

"A really pretty scarf," Faith said. "It's pure silk and it's got all these wild, swirling colors."

"Sounds like Winnie," KC said.

Faith was encouraged. At least KC was showing some interest. "Melissa and Lauren are setting up the decorations right now," Faith informed her, "and after I leave here I'm going to pick up the food."

"Oh, I couldn't eat anything right before the tea," KC said, pacing back and forth across the room.

"Well, you don't have to eat or drink anything if you don't want to. All I ask is that you show up.

Five minutes," Faith begged. "That's all I ask. Do it for Winnie or do it for me, but just do it. Please. Winnie is falling to pieces. If she saw your face, if you smiled and said hello, it would mean so much to her."

"I can't promise anything," KC said. "I mean, I hear what you're saying and I feel sorry for her and everything, but even five minutes could make a big difference in how I look for this tea. I don't even know what I'm going to wear yet."

"Don't you have any ideas?" Faith asked.

KC lifted a strand of pearls from her desk. "Lauren lent me these," she said. "They're the only thing I'm definitely wearing, but I don't think they're quite enough on their own."

Faith laughed. "Maybe not, but you'd certainly make an unforgettable impression if you walked into the sorority house wearing nothing but Lauren's pearls." Faith knelt on the floor and picked up a red silk blouse and plaid wool skirt. "How about this?" she suggested. "That's always looked nice on you."

"That's the problem," KC said. "Everything here has always looked nice on me because I've worn it all ten million times."

Faith rose. "KC, no matter what you wear, I'm sure you'll look beautiful. You always do."

KC smiled nervously.

"Brooks should be bringing Winnie by Coleridge Hall at two-thirty. Your tea's not until four o'clock. Just stand there while we shout surprise, wish her a happy birthday, then go. Okay?"

KC heaved a huge sigh. "Okay."

"You promise?"

KC bit her lip. "I promise," she said.

"Come around twenty after two," Faith said, heading for KC's door.

KC, already kneeling on the floor by the red blouse and plaid skirt, nodded.

"See you later," Faith said. "Good luck." She carefully closed the door behind her.

"What time is it?" Faith asked, pacing back and forth across the common room.

"Seventeen after two," Melissa answered. "Exactly one minute after the last time you asked." Melissa stood behind the refreshment table, lining up clear plastic cups in symmetrical rows.

"Where *is* everybody?" Faith worried, turning to Lauren. "Isn't Dash coming?"

Lauren, perched on the arm of a leatherette couch, listlessly swung a purple party hat by its elastic chin strap. "He, uh, was busy this afternoon. Staff meeting, I think."

"What about the rest of the people from our dorm?" Faith asked.

"I don't know," Lauren said glumly. "I invited everybody, but a lot of them had classes."

"I'm going to be late for practice as it is," said Melissa. "Not that it matters much anymore."

"Well, we'll just have to act like more of a crowd," said Kimberly Dayton, Faith's next door neighbor. Kimberly, a slender black girl, was a dance major. Her hair was in a bun, and she wore a long red sweater over black tights, red-and-black striped legwarmers, and ankle-high black boots. "With Freya here, we can certainly *sound* like more of a crowd."

Freya, Kimberly's roommate, smiled. "Happy birthday tooooooo yoooooooou!" she sang in a loud, operatic soprano. Blond, blue-eyed Freya was an opera major from Germany.

"We need more people!" Faith insisted, her forehead wrinkling.

There was the sound of footsteps in the hall. All heads turned expectantly toward the door. Two tall, muscular young men entered. One was tan with shaggy blond hair and wore jeans with a ripped T-shirt that said Malibu. The other was olive-skinned with short, dark, curly hair.

"Is this where the party is?" the blond guy asked.

"We *love* a good party," the dark-haired one agreed. "Par-*ty!* Par-*ty!* Par-*ty!*"

"Don't mind him," the blond one said. Then he looked around. "Hey, where is everybody?"

"Come on in," Faith said, using her friendliest voice. They weren't exactly her idea of scintillating company, but at least they were bodies to fill up the room. "There's plenty to eat and drink. We've got a six-foot hero—"

"All *right,*" said the dark-haired guy.

The blond paused on his way to the refreshment table, turning back to Faith. "My name's Steve," he said, "and this is my good buddy Eric."

"We live downstairs from Winnie," Eric added, "in case you thought we were crashing."

"Of course not!" Faith said. "Help yourselves to anything you want."

There was the sound of more footsteps. Again, everyone turned toward the door, but this time a tall, skinny girl walked by, her head buried in a book.

"What time is it?" Faith asked again.

"Two twenty-two," Melissa said mechanically.

"Where's KC?" Faith asked frantically. "She said she'd be here!"

"She'll be here," Lauren reassured her. "She promised."

"How about some music?" Eric suggested. "It's sort of dead in here, if you don't mind my saying so."

"I've got some tapes!" Freya said. "Gian Carlo Menotti's *The Medium,* a tragic modern opera about a woman who holds seances."

"How about some Stones?" Eric said.

"It's two twenty-five," Melissa said, without being asked.

"KC's not coming!" Faith said, half to herself, half to Lauren. "I can't believe she lied to me. Winnie's going to be so upset."

There was a light, pattering sound at the window. Faith ran to it and lifted the closed shade just high enough to look outside. She saw a purple head of hair directly beneath her, entering the building. A few feet from the entrance, Brooks stooped down, picked up something from the ground, then threw another handful of pebbles at the window.

"They're coming!" Faith said. "Everybody hide!"

Lauren turned out the lights, closed the common-room door, then knelt behind the leatherette couch.

"I want a big 'surprise,' everybody," Faith directed her cast as she lifted the paper tablecloth and crawled under the table. As she waited in the dark amid the dust bunnies, she crossed her fingers.

Please let this party cheer Winnie up, she prayed. *Please don't let her notice how few people are here. Please let KC show up any minute.* Faith squeezed her crossed fingers extra hard on that last thought.

Then she listened through the silence. There was the sound of approaching footsteps. Faith lifted the tablecloth so she could see, her heart beating so loudly she was sure Winnie would hear it.

"Faith?" Brooks called as the doorknob turned.

The door opened, and Faith recognized the spiky silhouette of Winnie's hair.

"Surprise!" everybody yelled as Brooks turned on the lights.

Winnie blinked in the light as she looked around the room.

"Happy birthday, Winnie!" Faith said, jumping out from under the table and running over to give her friend a hug.

Winnie looked dazed. "Is this a party?" she asked.

Faith nodded. "And it's all for you."

"Where are all the people?" Winnie asked, her lower lip quivering.

"Oh, lots more people will be coming later," Faith said, hoping her words would come true.

Tears sprang to Winnie's eyes. "I notice KC couldn't make it."

Faith let out an anguished sigh, not knowing how to respond.

"She didn't want to come, right?" Winnie said, her voice quivering, tears spilling down her cheeks one after the other.

"She did!" Faith protested. "I just spoke to her an hour ago. I'm sure she'll be here any minute."

"No, she won't," Winnie whispered. Then a choked sob erupted from her throat. She tore herself away from Faith and raced out of the room.

"Knock, knock!" called a female voice from outside KC's room, accompanied by a light tap on the door.

"Faith?" KC answered. "Don't yell at me. I'm on my way."

KC, her hair slicked back into a neat braid, her makeup freshly applied, checked herself one last time in the mirror. She wore a white cotton blouse, open at the neck to reveal Lauren's pearls, and a beige, brown, and white plaid skirt. It wasn't the outfit she'd envisioned wearing at the sorority tea, but it would have to do.

KC ran to open the door.

It wasn't Faith who stood in the hall. It was Marielle.

"Oh, hi!" KC said, surprised. "What are you doing here?"

"I hope I'm not interrupting anything," Marielle said, reaching down to pick up a picnic cooler. As Marielle leaned down, KC saw that she also had a garment bag slung over her shoulder.

"What's all this?" KC asked as Marielle strode into KC's room.

"It's a secret," Marielle said conspiratorially as KC shut the door. "What I say and do here can never leave this room. You've got to promise."

"If I tell, may I never be a Tri Beta," KC said solemnly, raising her right hand.

Marielle's bright red lips parted in a smile. "That's what I wanted to hear. Now, I thought you might like a little help getting ready for the tea this afternoon. I mean, I know you have beautiful clothes, but I brought over a few of mine, just in case you wanted to wear something different."

KC couldn't believe her luck. It was as if Marielle were her fairy godmother, making her dreams come true. KC could hardly wait to see what was inside the garment bag, but it was already twenty after two. If she didn't leave right away for Faith's dorm, she wouldn't make it in time for Winnie's surprise. Maybe she could ask Marielle to wait in her room for ten minutes while she ran over.

But Marielle was already unzipping the bag. KC craned her neck to watch as Marielle removed first a deep lavender silk shirtwaist dress with mother-of-pearl buttons.

"Ooooh," KC sighed. Maybe she'd just let Marielle unpack, *then* she'd ask her to wait while she popped over to Coleridge Hall.

Marielle next removed a navy silk print blouse decorated with tiny white bows. The blouse had a matching skirt, nearly ankle-length, with pleats all the way around.

"I brought a couple of belts to go with this one," Marielle said, unzipping a side pocket and taking out a wide white leather belt with a heavy brass buckle. "Or you might want to try this one." She dipped into the side pocket again and pulled out a gold chain belt.

KC looked at her watch. It was already twenty-five after. Even if she left that moment, she'd miss the surprise. Faith was going to kill her! Even worse, Winnie might get even more depressed, and it would be all her fault. But what could she do? She wanted to get to the party as quickly as possible, but Marielle was being so generous. She couldn't be rude to her.

Marielle pulled out her third and last selection. It was a lightweight wool suit, jet black, with a cropped jacket and a skirt that stopped several inches above the knee. It had no lapels and was edged with wide white piping around the collar, hem, cuffs, and pockets. The jacket had large white fabric-covered buttons.

"That's gorgeous!" KC whispered. "I don't think I've ever seen you wear it before."

"It's brand-new," Marielle said. "I've never worn it. That's why I thought you might like to wear it for the tea. No one will recognize it."

"But Marielle," KC protested weakly, "that's too generous."

"Nonsense!" Marielle said. "This is a very big day for you. Where could I wear it that would be as important?"

"I don't know what to say," KC said, sitting down on her bed. "It's all incredibly beautiful. I don't know how I could possibly choose."

"Would you like to try them on?" Marielle offered.

"I would," KC said, "but I sort of have this other commitment."

"Right now?" Marielle asked. "Before the tea?"

"It's a surprise party at Coleridge Hall," KC said, "but I've already missed the surprise."

"Well, how about this," Marielle said. "After we choose your outfit, I'll drop you off there and wait while you run in. Then we can go over to the house."

KC bit her lip.

"Don't worry," Marielle said. "You'll get there." She picked up the lavender dress. "Now," she said, "I have a feeling it's going to be the black suit, but let's start with this."

As KC started to unbutton her blouse, Marielle removed the cover of the picnic cooler. KC saw that it was packed with ice, two bottles, and some clear plastic cups.

"What's that?" KC asked.

"That's the other part of the surprise," Marielle said. "It's something to help you relax. I figured you'd be really nervous before the tea."

"That's for sure," KC said, removing her blouse and hanging it on the back of her desk chair. "I don't think I slept more than an hour last night, and I couldn't eat a thing all day."

Marielle nodded wisely. "Just what I thought. This is the perfect antidote." She removed the first bottle, a liter of Coca-Cola. Then she lifted the second bottle out of the ice. It was a pint of rum.

"Rum?" KC asked, her eyes widening. "I, um, don't really drink. I mean, my parents don't drink anything stronger than carrot juice, so I never really had much experience . . ."

"There's nothing to it," Marielle said. "You get dressed, I'll pour." She dropped an ice cube in the glass, then poured some Coca-Cola.

Marielle waited until KC had slipped the lavender dress over her head before she poured a hefty dose of rum. Though the glass was almost full, Marielle poured in a few more drops of rum. "Here."

KC's head emerged through the neck of the lavender dress. "I don't know," KC said when she saw the drink. "I'm afraid of what could happen."

Marielle laughed. "Nothing's going to happen. It's just a weak rum and Coke. You'll feel a little calmer, that's all."

Still hesitant, KC accepted the glass and took a small sip. It tasted dark and sweet and syrupy. Not too different from a regular Coke, just a little heavier. "This isn't too bad," KC said.

"So what do you think of the dress?" Marielle asked.

"It feels so light and soft," KC said, running her fingers down her sides. "It almost feels as if I'm not wearing anything." KC took another sip. "And I look taller somehow."

"That's because it's all one color," Marielle said. "When you wear two separate pieces, it cuts your body in half."

KC took another sip before removing the dress. "Wow," she said, swishing the drink around inside her mouth, "I really am beginning to feel better."

Marielle smiled. "See?" she said kindly. "There wasn't anything to be afraid of. Try on the navy."

The navy outfit gave KC a different look—classic, tasteful, subdued—but KC liked that, too. She continued to sip.

"You do look wonderful," Marielle agreed.

KC giggled. "They say clothes make the man," she said. "I think they should revise that. Clothes make the *woman*. Or clothes make the man *and* woman, or clothes make the man-person and woman-person. That's more equal." She giggled again. "Okay, next candidate." She took another sip before putting down her almost-empty glass.

"I think we need a little refill," Marielle said, jumping up to get more rum and Coke from the cooler.

KC paid no attention to what Marielle was doing. She was too entranced by the sight of herself in the black suit. She was beginning to doubt if it really was just the clothes that made her look good. It had to be her own striking looks, too. Her gray eyes had a veiled, mysterious quality, her skin had a porcelain gleam, her lips a pouty softness.

KC struck a dramatic pose, sucking in her cheeks to make her cheekbones even more prominent. Then she threw her hands on her hips and began to cross the room. When she reached the door, she turned sharply the way she thought a runway model would, but she tripped and almost fell.

"Whoops!" KC said, giggling again. "I guess you have to train to be a model, like go to charm school or something. But it couldn't be *that* difficult. I mean, all they do is walk around with books on their heads, right?"

KC stumbled toward her desk and removed a thesaurus. "This should be the right size." She balanced the volume on her head, but it immediately slipped off and fell on the floor. "Oh, well," KC said. "Plenty more where that came from." She picked up a dictionary, which also slid off, followed by an accounting textbook, a campus phone book, and a novel. Soon there was a pile of books at her feet.

"Silly idea," KC said, tripping over the books as she reached for the again-full glass of rum and Coke. "I didn't want to be a model anyway. Too smart for that. I've got my brains to get me places. And fry mends—I mean, my friends." She sat down beside Marielle, who was watching from the bed. "Marielle, you're the best friend I ever had. You come here, you bring me the clothes off your back, you help put me in the best mood. I don't know how I'll ever thank you."

"Believe me, KC, you already have," Marielle said, rising. "I'll just put the rest of my stuff away, then I'll drive you over to the house."

"That's so nice of you," KC said. "You're such a nice friend, you know that? You're really, really nice."

"Thank you," Marielle said, putting the bottles back in the cooler.

KC stood up quickly, then put a hand to her head. "Whoa!" she said. "Altitude change. The air's thinner up here."

"Okay, here's the deal," Marielle said as the girls headed for the hallway. "I'm going to drop you a couple of blocks from the house so no one knows you were with me. Then I'll park and meet you inside the house."

"Don't you want to be seen with me?" KC asked, her eyes filling with tears. "Aren't I good enough to get into the Tri Betas?"

"I just broke a very big Tri Beta rule by helping a potential pledge," Marielle explained. "We can't let anyone know that I was with you just now, or it could look really bad for both of us."

KC nodded. "Big secret," she said. "I won't say a thing. My mouth is sealed shut. Zipper lip."

"Very good," Marielle said again.

As Marielle watched KC stumble down the hallway ahead of her, she smiled in triumph. Her plan had worked perfectly. Now KC would pay for dumping those drinks on her and ratting on Mark about hazing that geeky freshman. Even better, Courtney would look bad when her special pet KC started acting like a drunken fool. Act one of Marielle's revenge had ended. Marielle couldn't wait for act two.

Twelve

"Too bad these aren't going anywhere," Winnie said as she and Melissa pedaled furiously, side by side, on the stationary bicycles. "I'd like to get so far away from here, no one would ever find me."

Melissa looked over at Winnie's bicycle and noticed she was doing level twelve, the highest and most difficult level, at an amazing speed.

"At the rate you're pedaling," Melissa said, "you're going to get there, too. Or else the bike will explode."

When Winnie had run out of the surprise party, Melissa had chased her all the way to the gym. Winnie had insisted that she had too much angry energy to trust herself anywhere else and wanted to work out her frustrations on the bike. Melissa couldn't leave Winnie alone in that state, even if it meant missing practice, so she decided she'd work out alongside her.

Winnie, who had a light weight in either hand, started pumping her arms furiously back and forth. "I hate my life!" she chanted in time to the rhythm of her legs and arms. "I hate my life! I hate my life! I hate my life! I mean, I know I'm not perfect, but I've tried to be a good person. So why isn't anybody there for me when I need them? Josh has forgotten I'm alive, and KC obviously feels the same way. You think they're trying to tell me something?"

"Don't worry about them," Melissa urged. "It's just a law of nature that you can't count on anybody but yourself. That's what Caitlin made me realize."

"Caitlin?" Winnie asked. "Who's she?"

"She's the best middle-distance runner on the team. She tried to warn me about Brooks, but I didn't listen. Now I wish I had, because she was right. Brooks was just trying to get what he needed out of me, but he could have cared less about what *I* needed."

"So here we are," Winnie panted, sweat pouring

down her forehead, "two islands of lonely self-sufficiency."

"It's better than letting someone get too close," Melissa said. "You can get used to being alone."

"I don't know," Winnie said. "I've felt alone for weeks, and the feeling's only getting worse." Winnie ran a hand through her sweaty purple hair. "Only seven people managed to make it to my surprise party. Actually only five, because Eric and Steve were only there for the free food. Yup, you can call me Miss Popularity."

"It was a bad time for a party," Melissa said. "That's the only reason there were so few people. A lot of others wanted to come, but they had classes."

"Not KC," Winnie said. "She didn't want to come." Winnie stopped pedaling. "Forty-eight minutes at level twelve," she said. "Not bad for a nonathlete."

"Not bad for anyone," Melissa said as she, too, came to the end of her program.

"Are you done?" Winnie asked. "I am."

"I'm going for twenty-four more," Melissa said.

"You're an animal," Winnie said.

"I wasn't pedaling at level twelve," Melissa answered. "I've still got a few ounces of energy left."

"I'm going to the sauna," Winnie said. "And if

it's hot enough, I'm going to let myself shrivel up like a prune. Then KC and Josh will be sorry."

"You'll be sorrier," Melissa said. "Go easy, okay?" Melissa punched in her next program on the bicycle's control panel. "See you later."

Winnie headed for her locker, where she peeled off her sweaty T-shirt and bicycle shorts. Then she grabbed two towels, wrapped one around her body and the other around her purple hair, and headed for the sauna.

The warm smell of cedar enveloped her as she opened the door to the sauna. She was in luck. It was empty. Winnie climbed to the top level and lay down. It was peaceful and quiet and warm. Maybe she would just lie there until she dried up into a little pile of ashes. Winnie closed her eyes.

She heard the door open, but she didn't bother to open her eyes.

"Ooh, nice," said a girl's voice. Winnie felt vibrations as someone lay down on the bench beneath her.

"My legs can really use this heat," said another girl. Winnie heard her lie down across the room. "Terry was a maniac this afternoon."

Terry? Wasn't that Melissa's track coach? Winnie opened her eyes and saw two girls lying on the lowest level. The one directly below her had frizzy brown hair and a long, thin face. The girl on the other side of the sauna was black, with braided hair and powerful-looking legs. They were probably Melissa's teammates.

"Hey, Demi," said the brown-haired girl. "Did you notice who was missing from practice this afternoon? Looks like my plan is working." She grinned.

"You're terrible, Caitlin, you know that?" said Demi. "Why don't you give the girl a break?"

Caitlin? Winnie's eyes opened even wider. That was the girl Melissa had mentioned, her friend from the team. Melissa had missed practice that day, though she was working out on her own. Could they be talking about Melissa? And what did Caitlin mean by her 'plan'?

Caitlin grew serious. "We're here to win, right? And who says it's all got to come from our bodies? The mind's the most powerful muscle we've got. I'm just using mine, that's all."

"You're psyching the poor girl out, that's what you're doing," Demi said. "And it's not fair."

"What's not fair about it?" Caitlin asked. "Melissa's got the advantage over me in every other way. I'm just trying to even things out a little bit. And doing a very good job, if I may add."

"You've turned her into a nervous wreck," Demi said. "Is that really what you want?"

"Look," Caitlin said, "I didn't tell her anything that wasn't true. If you want to be a top athlete, you've got to make sacrifices, and a personal life is the first thing that's got to go."

"For you, maybe," Demi said, "but not for me. I've got my man, and I'm not letting him go."

"Well, it's easier for you," Caitlin said. "Jeff is on the men's track team, so you're both going through the same thing."

"And we pull each other through," Demi added. "If he weren't there for me, I don't know how I'd make it. And anyway, having a boyfriend's not really the point. You just wanted to mess with Melissa's mind because you were scared she'd beat you."

Caitlin tensed. "It's taken me almost three years to break one fifty-one in the eight hundred meters, and Melissa might do it her freshman year. Do you know how that feels? When you want something so badly it hurts and you work and work to get it, then some kid comes along who doesn't even care as much and gets it without even trying?"

"She tries," Demi said. "She tries hard."

"But running doesn't matter to her the way it matters to me," Caitlin said. "She wants to be a doctor. This is just a sideline for her. For me, it's my whole life. So I just introduced a few negative thoughts into her brain. So what? She did the rest.

But I have to admit, it's sort of fun watching her psych herself out. She's really been screwing up at practice, she broke up with her boyfriend, and now Terry's threatening not to let her start at the next meet."

Winnie was getting dizzy, and it wasn't from the heat. So that was why Melissa's life had been going crazy lately. It was because of that girl! A jealous, mean-spirited, desperate girl who didn't care how she hurt Melissa as long as she could win her stupid race. Yes, Melissa wanted to be a doctor—and her whole education depended on her track scholarship. And Brooks—Winnie knew Brooks was the first person in Melissa's life who'd ever been totally there for her, totally supportive. She knew how happy Melissa had been, how her hard shell had finally started to crumble. She knew exactly how Melissa had felt because Winnie had felt the same way with Josh. Her shell had been a different one: flakiness, flirtatiousness, trying to act more experienced with men than she really was. But Josh had done the same thing for her—opened her up, helped her relax, made her realize she didn't have to try so hard to be loved.

Well, it may be too late for me to save my own relationship, Winnie thought, *but I'm not going to lie here a second longer when there's still a chance I can straighten out Melissa's.* It took every ounce of self-control Winnie had to make herself sit up slowly and exit the sauna without screaming. But as soon as the door closed behind her, Winnie threw on her clothes and ran as fast as she could to find Melissa.

"Would you like another drink?" the freshman asked politely. KC looked up at the Tri Beta sister leaning over her with a pitcher of lemonade. There was something wrong with the girl. Her brown hair, held back by a headband, seemed to have no edges. Her face looked distorted, as if she were under water.

"You should see a doctor," KC told the girl. "He'll fix you up right away."

"I beg your pardon?" asked the girl in long, drawn-out syllables.

KC turned to the other girls who sat scattered around the Tri Beta living room in a loose circle. They, too, looked out of focus. They were a blur of pastel colors, headbands, and pearls. By the fireplace, sitting in her high-backed leather armchair like a queen on her throne, was Courtney Conner, president of the Tri Betas.

"Maybe it's me," KC said loudly to everyone. "Maybe I ought to get my glasses checked." She felt for her eyes, then laughed. "Oh yeah! That's right! I don't wear glasses!"

A blond girl sitting to KC's left placed a gentle hand on her arm. "So tell me, KC," she said, "what are some of your beauty secrets? I'm sure everyone here has admired your picture in the calendar and is dying to know."

"My beauty secrets?" asked KC, cocking her head to one side. "That's a very interesting question. Well, I would have to say carrots, mostly. Carrots and cucumbers."

"Oh really?" asked the girl. "What do you do with them? Slice them and put them on your eyelids?"

"Well, carrots *are* good for your eyes," KC said. "Any rabbit knows that. Bugs Bunny doesn't wear glasses, either, does he? But no—no, no, no. We don't wear carrots. We eat them. Or we drink them. My parents make a really great carrot juice in their restaurant. It's just full of vitamins, but one time— this was really funny!—my mother forgot to put the top on the juicer, and these little carrot shreds went flying all over the restaurant and sprayed all the customers. It was as if a carrot bomb had gone off!"

KC started laughing, expecting the sorority sisters to join in. After several seconds, though, she realized she was laughing alone. The girls around her weren't even smiling. They were just staring at her as if she were crazy.

Courtney rose from her armchair by the fireplace and approached KC's chair. "KC," she said in her smooth, gracious voice, "why don't we get you a cup of coffee in the kitchen?"

Rising meekly, KC followed the Tri Beta president out of the room, conscious that everyone was staring at her as if she had two heads. As soon as KC had passed through the archway into the kitchen, Courtney turned to face her.

"It seems," Courtney said, "that you've had something more to drink this afternoon than just carrot juice."

KC looked at her blankly. "Huh?"

"I could understand an occasional glass of wine if you're over twenty-one," Courtney said, "but that doesn't seem to be the case here."

"What are you talking about, Courtney? I'm not drunk. I mean—oh, no!"

Courtney's clear blue eyes were as cold as ice. "After all I've done for you, KC . . ." Her voice drifted off, and at the same time KC felt the curtain of fog slowly begin to drop away from around her.

Marielle had done it. She had paid KC back, and royally. She hadn't come to KC's room to bring clothes and be supportive; she had come to get her drunk, so KC would embarrass herself at the sorority tea. And KC had been so desperate, it had worked like a charm. All the Tri Betas were laughing at her, and Courtney had pretty much told her she wasn't Tri Beta material. She'd blown it. As usual.

At that moment Marielle passed by the kitchen door and looked in. When she saw Courtney and KC together, she smiled innocently and waved hello.

Thirteen

Melissa was running for her life. At least, that was the way it felt to her. She could almost imagine demons snapping at her heels, trying to drag her down. The demons all had Caitlin's face. They were trying to stop her from seeing Brooks again, but this time Melissa was going to outrun them.

As Melissa poured on a surge of speed, racing across the campus toward Brooks's dorm, she felt renewed confidence. She was a strong runner, a great runner, and she always had been. She ran toward Rapids Hall as if she were running in the Olympics.

Unconscious of her sweaty clothes and disheveled hair, Melissa dashed up the steps of Brooks's dorm two at a time and flung open the door. Then she zoomed down the hall and pounded on Brooks's door. He had to be home. He just had to be. And if he wasn't, she'd find him, wherever he was, no matter how long it took.

Brooks opened the door. When he saw Melissa, he started to close it again, but she pushed against it with her hand.

"Please, Brooks," she begged. "I just want to talk to you."

"I thought you didn't have time to talk," Brooks said. "Shouldn't you be at practice right now? Or memorizing chemistry tables or something?"

"This is where I want to be," Melissa said. "With you."

"I doubt that," Brooks said. He stared down at the floor.

"I'm sorry," Melissa said after a long silence. "I'm sorry about a lot of things. Couldn't I come in for just a minute and talk to you?"

"Where were you when *I* wanted to talk?" Brooks mumbled.

"I know I wasn't there before," Melissa said. "But I am now. And if you're busy right this second, I'll meet you anywhere you say. In the dining commons, on the green, at the track, even at the minia-ture-golf course."

"What would be the purpose?" Brooks asked.

"I'd like to start again," Melissa said simply. She was too desperate to be defensive or coy. "You're the best thing that's ever happened to me."

"Mel," Brooks sighed. "I'm not going to set my-self up to be hurt again."

"Brooks!" Melissa pleaded.

"Sorry. I can't do this again." He started to shut the door.

"Please!" Melissa begged, but the door closed firmly and she heard the lock click.

Melissa waited a moment in the hall. But the door stayed closed and all she heard was a radio turned on inside the room, blaring loud rock mu-sic. Melissa had run fast, but not fast enough.

Faith had never run so fast in her entire life. Her legs were aching, her chest felt tight, and she could barely breathe, but the anger she felt inside kept her going. After everything she'd done to keep her friends together, after years of playing peacemaker between Winnie and KC, after all the planning she'd done for Winnie's surprise party, the whole thing had exploded in her face.

After Winnie had run out, Faith had raced over

to Langston House to find KC and chew her out for missing the party. But KC had already gone to the sorority tea. That's what KC's next-door neighbor had told Faith. The neighbor had said that KC spent the afternoon with Marielle Danner and they'd left the dorm together a little before four o'clock.

So that was the kind of friend KC wanted now? A back-stabbing snob like Marielle? Was KC so mesmerized by Marielle's money that she had forgotten about her old friends? KC had done a lot of things in the past that Faith didn't approve of, but she'd never broken a promise before. And she'd never done anything so blatantly cruel to Winnie. Faith might have forgiven her before, but this time she was going to tell KC exactly what she thought. No more being sweet, nice, maternal, friend-to-everyone Faith. Faith was finally going to give KC a piece of her mind, and she didn't care how many sorority sisters were watching.

Gasping for breath, Faith reached Greek Row, the residential street of fraternities and sororities. Tri Beta was just down the block. Faith slowed to a walk so she could get enough breath back to yell. Arms swinging vigorously, she strode along the sidewalk and up the path to the Tri Beta house.

The door was open. Without bothering to

knock, Faith marched inside. The entrance hall was spacious, with a wide staircase sweeping up to the second floor. Homey pastel rugs were scattered over the burnished wooden floor and oil paintings of Tri Beta alumnae hung at intervals along both sides of the wall.

Faith heard voices and followed the sound to a large colonial-style living room with a circle of leather armchairs and a fireplace at the far end. A bunch of pretty girls sat in the chairs, drinking lemonade and eating cookies. Faith spotted KC immediately. KC sat a little off to the side, drinking a cup of coffee and looking pale. Courtney Conner sat beside her.

Ignoring the stares of the Tri Betas, Faith walked right up to KC and planted herself right in front of her.

"Kahia Cayanne Angeletti!" Faith projected her voice as if she were on the stage of a theater filled with thousands of seats. "You are the lowest form of life I have ever encountered. You're certainly not a human being. A human being cares about other people. A human being remembers who her friends are and doesn't desert them when they're in trouble. A human being doesn't go around ruining someone's life and then kicking them while they're down."

KC stared up at Faith miserably. She didn't protest. She didn't even open her mouth. She just listened.

"You have absolutely destroyed Winnie," Faith continued. She didn't mind that the Tri Beta sisters were all listening eagerly to every word. "You gave me your word of honor that you would come to Winnie's birthday party, but obviously that's not worth anything anymore. All you had to do was show up for five minutes, but no! You'd rather spend the afternoon with Marielle Danner trying on clothes and doing your nails and who knows what else."

Courtney, who'd been watching Faith with a calm, steady gaze, suddenly sat up in her chair. "I beg your pardon," she said, "but what did you say?"

"You want me to repeat the whole thing?" Faith asked.

"No," Courtney said quietly. "Just that last part about Marielle."

"Excuse me," Marielle said, rising from her chair and heading for the front hall.

"Stay right where you are," Courtney commanded her.

Marielle stopped short and looked uncomfortably around the room.

"I said KC had spent the afternoon with Marielle," Faith said. "They were seen leaving the dorm together. And I'll bet Marielle lent her that suit, too, because I *know* it doesn't belong to KC."

"Is this true?" Courtney asked KC.

KC nodded without looking up.

"Marielle, KC," Courtney said, rising from her chair. "I'd like both of you to come with me to the kitchen, please. Faith, please come as well, if you like."

Faith followed curiously, knowing that every other girl in the room wished she could go, too. When the four of them were inside the kitchen, Courtney turned to Marielle.

"I want the truth," Courtney said. "If you lie to me, you'll only make it worse for yourself. Did you spend the afternoon in KC's room?"

Marielle nodded defiantly. "So I lent her some clothes. So what? You like her. You want her in. I was just helping her along."

"You know that's a violation of house rules," Courtney said. "That alone is grounds for expulsion. But that's not the part I'm most concerned about. I'm concerned about the fact that KC is drunk."

"Drunk?" Faith asked, her eyes widening in surprise. "KC? She's never had anything stronger than carrot juice in her entire life."

"Please don't talk about carrot juice," KC whispered, looking up. Tears were spilling over her high cheekbones and down her smooth cheeks.

"Did KC consume any alcohol while she was in your presence this afternoon?" Courtney asked.

Marielle didn't answer. Courtney looked at KC.

"Obviously," answered KC quietly.

"And where did she get that alcohol?" Courtney turned back to Marielle. "Did *you* provide it?"

Marielle gazed stubbornly at Courtney.

"If you do not answer," Courtney said, "I will expel you immediately."

"You'll expel me anyway," Marielle said, "so why should I tell you the truth?"

"So it *is* the truth," Courtney said.

Marielle shrugged. "I guess I have nothing to lose now. Yes, I gave her the drink. Two drinks, actually. Rum and Coke. But it wasn't as if I had to force it down her throat."

"You were drunk?" Faith asked KC. "Is that why you didn't come to the party?"

"I was just leaving when Marielle came in," KC said quietly. "She brought all these clothes with her, and a cooler. I didn't know what was going to happen. She said the drink was a weak one. She said it would help me relax."

"I know how tense you were," Faith remembered.

"Knowing Marielle, I'd be surprised if there was any Coke in that drink at all," Courtney said. "Marielle, I am placing you under probation. You are not to participate in any sorority functions until I assemble a tribunal to hear your case."

"Don't you want to read me my rights?" Marielle asked.

"This is not a joking matter," Courtney said. "I plan to have you voted out of the Tri Betas. You'd better start making phone calls and figure out where you're going to live because it certainly won't be here."

Marielle glared at Courtney with undisguised hatred. "You think you're so great, don't you, Courtney? Little Miss Perfect with the perfect hair and the perfect voice, admired by all for her courtesy and quiet good taste. Well, you know what, Courtney? You make me sick."

"Are you quite finished?" Courtney asked.

"No, I'm not," Marielle said. She turned to KC. "And *you* don't fool anybody. You think you can buy a velvet jacket and trick us into believing you're sorority material? You don't have any breeding, and it's obvious you don't have any money."

Courtney placed a protective arm around KC. "I

wouldn't speak that way to her if I were you," she said. "Whatever KC's background may be, it certainly won't limit her as far as we're concerned. As for this incident, we won't hold KC responsible since it was obviously not of her making."

" 'Obviously not of her making,' " Marielle mimicked in a whiny voice. "I don't know why you even bothered to invite her to the tea since it's clear you're going to make sure she gets in anyway. I'm not sitting before your stupid tribunal, and you can't make me. I'm out of here, Courtney. I'll send for my things."

Marielle turned sharply away from Courtney and stormed out the kitchen door, her sleek brown hair flapping behind her.

Fourteen

Lauren stared at the empty blue screen on her computer monitor, as she'd been doing for the past half-hour. She had a creative-writing assignment due the next day, but her mind was as blank as the screen. The topic was "truth." Lauren's professor hadn't been more specific than that. All she'd said was to fill up two pages with anything that came to mind.

Something actually did come to mind when Lauren thought of the word *truth*, but it was still too painful to write about. She thought about Dash, about how well their relationship had been going until she realized it was all founded on a lie.

She thought about how she'd assumed that she knew him and loved him for who he was, only to find out he was someone else. She thought about how he'd made her feel guilty for being rich when his family was upper-middle-class. She thought about how angry he'd made her . . . and how much she missed him.

Lauren stared at the phone on her desk. Half of her wanted to pick up the receiver and dial his room, the other half was willing the phone to ring. She wasn't going to be the one to make the first move. He was the one who'd lied. Let him make the effort to mend things. Of course, if she didn't call him, she might never speak to him again. It had already been three days and she hadn't heard a word.

Truth. Lauren continued staring at the empty screen, so lost in her thoughts that she almost didn't hear the soft tap on the door. The tapping grew louder.

"Is someone there?" she called.

There was another tap.

Sighing, Lauren rose from her chair. When she opened the door, she found herself staring at the top of a head covered with a red bandanna. It was Dash, and he seemed fascinated by the dirty shoelaces of his high-top sneakers. It took all Lauren's strength to hide how glad she was to see him.

"I see you're back in costume," Lauren said sternly. "You don't have to pretend with me anymore, Dash. I know who you really are, remember?"

"Maybe I wasn't pretending," Dash said, raising his dark eyes to meet hers. "Maybe you just assumed the wrong thing."

Lauren rolled her eyes. "Maybe you *led* me to assume the wrong thing."

"Maybe you were predisposed to believe certain things about me," Dash argued.

"Maybe you should come inside," Lauren said, "so everyone in Coleridge Hall doesn't get a repeat performance of the show we put on outside the restaurant."

"Maybe I will," Dash said, pressing his lips together. Lauren thought she saw a smile almost escape, but she could have been mistaken.

Lauren closed the door behind them and sat in her desk chair so she wouldn't have to sit next to him on the bed. Angry as she was, she didn't know how long she could hold out if she was physically close to him. Already she could barely suppress the urge to throw her arms around him. But she was determined to stay mad, at least until he apologized.

"Where were we?" Dash asked, staring at her with bright eyes.

"You were accusing me of having false preconceptions about your family," Lauren reminded him.

"Oh, yeah, that's right. Well, didn't you? Didn't you think that just because I was Latino, my family was some poor group of immigrants who barely spoke English?"

"Your mother *did* write to you in Spanish," Lauren argued. "You walk around here with your bandanna and your high-top sneakers and your sloppy clothes, so it's no wonder people have the impression you're a street kid. It has nothing to do with your ethnic background."

"Sure it does," Dash said. "If I had blond hair and blue eyes and dressed like this, people would just assume I was a slob, not necessarily poor."

"That may be true," Lauren admitted, "but you haven't exactly advertised the fact that you have expensive suits hanging in your closet and affluent parents paying your tuition. In fact, you've done everything in your power to hide it."

"Okay, okay, so I haven't exactly been forthcoming," Dash said. "You happy now? I admit it. My dad makes money. So does my mom. But how far do you think I'd get as a campus radical if I wore my navy blue blazer, gray flannel pants, and tasseled loafers?"

"I guess it's not exactly my picture of a revolutionary," Lauren said. A chuckle started up her throat, but she squelched it. She was still mad at him, or she was supposed to be.

"I know appearances aren't supposed to matter," Dash continued, "but I just thought the people I work with would take me more seriously if they thought I came from a struggling family."

"I guess I understand your point," Lauren said, "and you're free to dress any way you want. But the thing that makes me even madder is that you made *me* feel so guilty about being rich." Lauren's anger was beginning to return. "That wasn't fair. And it was the height of hypocrisy."

Dash looked down at his shoelaces again. "I guess it is, isn't it?" he said softly. "It's doubly hypocritical because I was calling *you* a hypocrite."

"Which I'm not," Lauren said. "I'd never try to pretend to be something I'm not."

Dash looked up again, his eyes gleaming, a smile playing on his lips. "Oh, yeah?" he challenged her. "What about that rag of a dress you wore to the restaurant to meet my parents? You thought my family was poor, so you were trying to dress down when you met them."

Lauren bit her lip and stared at the ceiling. "Oh, yeah."

"Gotcha!" Dash said, pointing a finger at her and grinning.

"Well, I wouldn't have dressed that way if you'd told me the truth," Lauren said. "And it's a shame you've kept your family a secret because they're really pretty nice."

Dash mumbled something.

"What was that?" Lauren asked.

"I said they are, aren't they?" Dash admitted. "Money or no money, they're good people. My sister's going to be a public defender when she gets out of law school, and my mother started a program that sends a hospital van to poor neighborhoods to provide free medical care."

"See?" Lauren said. "They're not so terrible."

"They liked you, by the way," Dash said. "Don't ask me why."

"I was *charming!*" Lauren exclaimed.

"And well-dressed, too," Dash said. He started laughing, showing his even white teeth. "What was that, your poverty outfit?"

"There was nothing wrong with that dress,"

Lauren said, pretending to be offended. "And by the way, it wasn't a rag, it was merely plain."

"Plain awful," Dash said.

"Don't make me angry, Dash Ramirez, or—"

"Or what?" Dash said, gazing at her intently with a sexy grin. "What are you going to do to me?"

"You don't want to know," Lauren said. "It's too horrifying to describe."

"I think I can handle it," Dash said. "Give me your best shot."

Lauren rose from her chair. "You'll be sorry," she sang as she leaped on the bed and began to tickle his stomach.

"Stop!" Dash cried for real, laughing uncontrollably. "That's my most vulnerable spot. Stop! Please!"

"Say you loved the dress!" Lauren demanded. "Say it was the most beautiful dress you ever laid eyes on."

"Never!" Dash said, groaning even while he laughed.

"Say it!" Lauren insisted, keeping at it until he was curled up into a ball, his arms clamped protectively around his knees. Then, suddenly, before she knew he'd done it, he'd flipped her over and was looking down at her.

"Say it," she said softly, gazing up at him.

Dash stared down at her with loving eyes. "It was

a beautiful dress," he said quietly, "on a beautiful girl. And I'm sorry we had a fight."

"I'm sorry, too," Lauren said. "I missed you."

"I missed you, too."

"I guess we've got a lot to learn about each other, don't we?" Lauren asked.

Dash nodded. "But I'm a very complicated person. If you want to know the real me, it will take some time."

"I'm in no hurry," Lauren whispered. "And there's a lot I've never told you about myself."

Dash raised his eyebrows. "With so much to learn, we'd better start soon."

"Where shall we begin?" Lauren asked.

Dash let go of her arms, but Lauren didn't try to get up. She just closed her eyes as he leaned toward her and kissed her gently, then passionately.

Fifteen

Faith covered up the map and tried to name all the regions in the Ottoman Empire. Wallachia, Anatolia, Mesopotamia, Syria. She racked her brain, but couldn't come up with any more. She knew she'd have to do better than that on her Western Civ quiz the next day. She uncovered the map and slapped a hand to her forehead. Of course! Moldavia, Albania, Serbia . . . most of them ended in *ia*. Maybe she could make up a rhyme to help herself remember.

"Yo, Faith!" called a familiar voice outside in the hall. "You home?"

Faith got up from her desk and opened the door.

Winnie stood outside. Her purple hair had faded to a pinkish mauve with brown roots. For the first time in several weeks, her T-shirt actually matched her pants, mainly because they were both black.

"Is this the new, subdued Winnie?" Faith asked, smiling at her friend.

Winnie glanced at her clothing and shrugged. "Everything else was dirty," she said. "I hate black. It's so somber."

"Well, you've still got enough color in your hair to brighten up the outfit," Faith said. "You want to come in?"

"Oh, yeah," Winnie said. "I almost forgot the reason I came over. Can I borrow your notes for the Western Civ quiz tomorrow?"

"Well, I'm studying them right now, but maybe we can study together."

"Okay!" Winnie said, shuffling into Faith's room and flopping down on Faith's bed. "Where's Lauren?"

"Out with Dash," Faith said. "Again."

"Guess they made up," Winnie said. "That didn't take long."

"Their fight was so dumb in the first place," Faith said. "Who cares which one of them has money and which doesn't? The point is, they belong together."

"I wish it were so clear-cut for me and Josh." Winnie sighed.

"You'll figure it out," Faith said. "And if you don't end up with him, it will be someone even better."

"I doubt it," Winnie said. "He's as good as it gets." She rolled over and stared up at the ceiling. "So," she said, "can *you* name all the regions in the Ottoman Empire?"

Faith groaned. "I was just testing myself. Do we have to know the dates, like which ones were conquered before 1453 and which ones were seized later?"

"I'm the wrong person to ask," Winnie said. "I haven't exactly been paying attention in class this semester."

There was a knock on the door. "It's open!" Faith called.

KC popped her head in. "Hi," she said shyly. Then she saw Winnie lying on Faith's bed. "Oh, you're busy," she said. "I could come back."

Winnie turned her head at the sound of KC's voice. Then she turned her face back up to the ceiling.

"We're just studying for the Western Civ quiz tomorrow," Faith said. "You can join us, if you want."

"Actually," KC said, "that's the real reason I came. I wanted to borrow your Western Civ notes."

Faith knew KC didn't need to borrow her notes any more than Winnie did. They'd both come to her room for the company, and maybe it was more than a coincidence that they'd come at the same time. Maybe fate had brought them together so they could make up.

Faith tried to help fate along. "My notes have never been so popular," she said, "but since they're in use, you'll have to study with us."

"Oh." KC paused uncertainly in the doorway. "I don't want to interrupt anything."

"Winnie doesn't mind, do you, Winnie?" Faith asked.

Winnie shrugged. "They're not *my* notes."

"You can sit on Lauren's bed," Faith invited KC. "We were just trying to figure out if we had to know when the regions in the Ottoman Empire became part of the empire."

KC sat down on Lauren's bed, her back stiff and straight, her hands folded in her lap.

"Make yourself at home, KC," Faith said.

"I don't feel too comfortable right now," KC began.

"I'll leave," Winnie said, pulling herself up to a sitting position.

"No," KC said. "That wasn't what I meant. I mean, I'm glad you're here, because I owe you an apology."

"Oh?" Winnie cocked one eyebrow. "Did you do something wrong?"

"Don't act like that, Win," KC said. "You're not making it any easier on me."

"Did you make *my* life any easier these past few weeks?" Winnie challenged her.

"No," KC admitted. "I created the problem, then I made it worse. There. Are you satisfied? I never should have opened my mouth to Josh and I should have been more supportive while you were depressed, and most of all I'm sorry I didn't come to your birthday party. I was planning to come. I honestly was, but Marielle sort of, uh, sidetracked me."

"I heard all about Marielle," Winnie said, "and I tried to warn you about her. You never should have trusted her in the first place."

"I know," KC said, "but I got carried away. If nothing else, though, it made me appreciate what real friends are. And it made me realize that it doesn't have to be all or nothing. I can be in Tri Beta without giving up my old friends—that is, if they haven't already given me up."

"So you think that now you've made that .heart-warming speech I'm supposed to just open up and forgive you?" Winnie asked. "You think just because you've decided you're ready to be friends again I'm going to jump right back in and trust you again?"

Winnie gazed at KC with a hardness in her eyes that Faith had never seen before. It scared her. Even when Winnie had been upset in the past, she'd never been so self-protective or difficult to read. What was going on inside that purple head of hers?

KC grabbed a curl hanging by her shoulder and twisted it around her finger. "I'm not asking you to jump back in," she said, intently studying her finger and the curl. "I'm just asking if there's a possibility, at some point in the future, of our being friends again."

Winnie shrugged. "Nothing's impossible."

KC gave her a grateful look.

"Don't get your hopes up," Winnie said. "It's just a cliché."

KC's face fell.

"I don't see how I can possibly forget what you did to me," Winnie said, "since I'm constantly reminded of it. Every time I walk down the hall of my dorm I see Josh with the same blond girl on his arm."

"Winnie, I'm sorry!" KC said. "Is there any way I can make it up to you?"

"I'm in such a bad slump right now, there's nothing you or anyone else can do to get me out," Winnie said. "I can't concentrate on any of my classes, I cry sometimes for no reason, and I just can't get excited about anything."

"That is bad," KC agreed. "You'd usually get excited over anything—a new pair of orange and green and purple striped shoes, a cute guy you never even met, a new flavor of ice cream at the grocery store . . ."

Winnie shrugged. "Don't worry about it. My mother would say it's just a phase. Meanwhile, I'll probably spontaneously combust. I wonder how she'd explain that."

"She'd be pretty upset," KC said. "And so would I."

Faith smiled. While KC and Winnie hadn't exactly made up, at least they were talking to each other. That was a start. She was happy that they'd done most of it without her. She hoped they'd be able to keep it up, too, because soon she wouldn't have any time to play peacemaker. Her job as a gofer on the film was starting soon and she might not even have enough time for her other classes, let alone her friends.

* * *

Melissa closed her eyes and screened out the red oval track, the cheering fans, and the seven other runners staggered behind her. She screened out thoughts of Caitlin and Terry and her scholarship. The only image she allowed in her mind was that of the white tape waiting for her at the finish line. The white tape that would break across her chest as she flew past Caitlin, Jamie, Mathilda, and the opposing runners from Winfield College.

Melissa opened her eyes and took one last look around. That was when she heard someone call her name. "You can do it, Melissa!"

It was Brooks, standing up at the top of the bleachers.

Melissa wasn't sure what to think. Maybe there was still a chance for them after all. Maybe she could start over with him, without the burden of all those Caitlin-inspired anxieties. There *had* to be a way to start again. Even thinking of him made her feel supercharged with energy, like a rocket engine jet-fueled and ready to take off. She felt as if she could run to Mars if she had to.

"Runners, take your marks!" Terry called, cocking his pistol.

Melissa placed her left foot ahead of her right and took a deep breath.

BANG! The gunshot rang out in the warm spring

air and Melissa sprang forward, her legs pumping powerfully and evenly. She was on the outermost track, not the best place to start from, but at least she reached the first curve before anyone else. Taking advantage, she cut sharply across to the inside as she headed around to the first straightaway. She kept picturing Brooks waiting for her at the finish line, arms outstretched. She wasn't going to let anyone or anything keep her from getting to him first.

As always, Caitlin appeared from nowhere, passing Melissa on the outside and taking the lead. Melissa held herself in check. She wasn't going to make the same mistake she'd made in practice by trying to pass Caitlin early on. She just held her pace, her arms swinging forcefully, helping to carry her forward.

A Winfield runner in a yellow track suit came up on Melissa's right, also trying to pass. Melissa held steady, especially when she noticed the woman was already breathing heavily. She had probably come out too fast, but that wasn't Melissa's problem. She was running her own race and it didn't matter what anyone else was doing. It was just her, the track, and Brooks at the finish line.

When the bell rang, signaling the second lap, the runner in yellow had fallen behind and Melissa was only a few paces behind Caitlin. Caitlin still seemed strong, but Melissa had a lot left to give. She picked up her pace a little so that she was nearly on Caitlin's heels. She knew she could have passed Caitlin and still had a good kick, but she held herself back just a little longer. She was waiting for the final straightaway.

The final curve was approaching. Caitlin looked back once, aware of Melissa right behind her. Melissa could tell that Caitlin was nervous, but she didn't think about that, either. She wasn't running against Caitlin. She was running against herself.

As soon as she'd cleared the final curve, Melissa channeled every ounce of energy she had into her lower body. Her legs were a blur as she shot forward on Caitlin's right and passed her, still picking up speed. She felt the wind whipping at her face as she trained her eyes on the white tape stretched taut across the track, waiting for her, beckoning to her, the only thing left between her and Brooks's arms.

The tape snapped in two as Melissa's chest broke through. The roar was deafening. Even though there were only a few hundred people in the stands, it sounded like much more, or maybe that was just because Melissa was so happy. She'd run the race she'd always known was in her. It just took some letting go to let it out. She'd never allowed herself to feel so relaxed, to stop analyzing her every move, to let her energy flow. And she owed most of that to Brooks, to the way he'd made her feel.

Melissa had run an extra lap before she realized she'd barely slowed down. When she reached the finish line again, Terry was waiting for her, waving his arms.

"Don't waste it!" he cried. "Save some of it for the next meet!"

Melissa smiled as she went into a light jog. Terry trotted along beside her.

"I guess you worked out whatever it was," Terry said tersely. "I hope your problem's solved."

How did everyone on the team know so much about what was going on inside her? It was uncanny. But, Melissa figured, Terry had been a coach for a long time. He'd probably seen it all.

"You want to know your time?" Terry asked.

Melissa smiled at him. "Under one fifty-one, right?"

Terry acted annoyed. "Pretty cocky for a freshman." Then he held up his stopwatch and Melissa stopped, still breathing hard.

The watch said one minute forty-nine point nine five seconds.

Melissa screamed. Then she screamed again. Terry pounded her on the back.

"You sure you want to go to med school?" he asked. "The Olympic trials are coming up."

Melissa shook her head. "This is good enough for me. I broke one fifty! I can't believe it!"

"Believe it," Terry said. Hanging his stopwatch around his neck with the other two, he trotted back to the center of the oval.

Out of the corner of her eye, Melissa spotted Caitlin stretching at the side of the track, but she didn't feel the need to gloat. She didn't even want to speak to her. She just wanted to find the one person in the world who'd made her feel good enough to run her best.

Brooks was leaning against the fence in the same spot where Melissa had seen him twice before. He wore his intramural soccer shirt with the sleeves rolled up to his elbows, displaying sturdy, muscular forearms. One leg of his faded jeans had a big rip, and his tanned knee showed through the tear.

Brooks was looking around, but he didn't seem excited. He just seemed worried and sad. Melissa's heart plummeted to her shoes. Had she been mistaken? Had she pumped up her hopes for no reason at all? Maybe he really *didn't* care about her anymore.

Melissa placed herself directly in front of Brooks. "Hi," she said.

"Hi." Brooks gave her a wan smile. "You ran a great race."

"Thanks," Melissa said. She studied his face, trying to guess what was going through his mind.

"So," Brooks said, "I guess you're wondering what I'm doing here."

Melissa looked up at him hopefully.

"Well," Brooks said, hanging his head and kicking at loose dirt with the toe of his hiking boot, "I felt bad that I made you mess up at practice the other day, so I wanted to come cheer you on."

"And?" Melissa asked, searching his face for more.

Brooks looked at her blankly.

"There wasn't anything else you wanted to tell me?" Melissa asked.

Brooks shook his head and flecks of sunlight danced on his golden curls. "I'm happy you won," he said. "And I wish you the best of luck for the rest of the semester."

So that was it? He'd come to the race only because he felt sorry for her? And after all they'd been through, all she'd learned, it was just going to end with him wishing her good luck?

"What about us?" Melissa asked, her eyes pained and anxious.

"There is no us," Brooks said simply. "Not anymore. You don't have time for a relationship, and I'll just have to get used to that. Of course, you could have chosen a different way to tell me."

"I'm sorry about that," Melissa said. "You don't know how sorry I am! All those things I said to you —I didn't know what I was talking about. I was just freaking out over track. It had nothing to do with you."

"That's nice to hear," Brooks said simply. "Well, see ya." He started to walk away.

"Wait!" Melissa called after him. "You don't understand."

"Please," Brooks said, "don't drag it out anymore. It's over, and I accept it."

Melissa's first impulse was to let him go, to accept his leaving as her punishment for treating him badly and letting herself be influenced by Caitlin. She deserved to be miserable without him for the rest of her life.

No! She wasn't a lonely island of self-sufficiency, as Winnie had described her. She couldn't be, not anymore. She wanted to love. To be loved. By Brooks.

"I love you!" Melissa shouted.

Brooks kept walking. For a moment Melissa was afraid he hadn't heard. Then, all of a sudden, he turned to face her.

"What did you say?" he asked, his face solemn.

"I love you, Brooks Baldwin," Melissa repeated. "Very, very much."

With a leap worthy of a long jumper, Brooks covered the distance between them and swept up Melissa in his arms.

"I love you, too," he whispered fiercely. "I love you, too."

Here's a sneak preview of Freshman Secrets, *the eighth book in the dramatic story of* FRESHMAN DORM.

Winnie had been staring at the downtown pavement for hours. The soles of her feet burned, and the back of her neck was sore. Her wet hair drooped into her eyes, and her sweater was soaked with rain.

She'd spent the previous night in the Greyhound bus station, watching the television that hung suspended on the wall and listening to the storm beat the side of the building. She'd slept a little, but mostly she'd just sat. Finally, at 5:00 A.M., the new ticket seller came on and chased her out.

Winnie hurried down the sidewalk. The wind howled, and the rain started again, drumming on the parked cars and trickling down her face. She tramped past darkened storefronts, junk shops, parking lots, rooming houses, and car dealerships. Now and then, someone passed her, but no one paid any attention.

Finally Winnie reached the north end of Springfield, where the dingy warehouses were replaced with glitzy hotels, designer shops, chic cafés and jewelry stores. Winnie spotted an awning and an open door. She dashed up the carpeted steps and stepped into the lobby of The Grandview Hotel. Quickly, she cut to the side of the lobby and slunk down in an overstuffed chair. The dampness of her clothes seeped into her skin, and she shivered.

Murmured voices echoed out of a nearby restaurant, and the faint sound of a string quartet drifted across the lobby. The chair she sat in was soft, deep, and comfortable. She let out a long sigh. She closed her eyes and started to drift off.

A tap on her shoulder woke her up.

"Excuse me, young lady."

Winnie squinted. A man was looming over her, wearing a dark blue uniform decorated with a gold braid and shiny buttons. His eyebrows were knitted with concern, and his voice was soft and kind. "I'm terribly sorry, but I can't allow you to sleep here," he announced.

Winnie breathed in, and a shiver ran down her back. Without saying a word, she stood up and walked out the lobby door.

She walked and walked, and her tears began to pour down, mixing with the misty rain. Okay, world! she felt like screaming. I get your message. There's nothing I can do and nowhere I can go. I'm getting the signal, loud and clear.

When Winnie walked past the darkened doorway of a used furniture store, she was only half conscious of a hissed whispering behind her. She crossed an empty street and stepped up onto a curb. She kept walking until she became aware that someone was following her. Someone was getting close. She heard the rustle of clothing. She heard the footsteps and felt someone put a hand on the back of her hair.

She tensed.

"Hey, baby," the voice said.

Winnie sped up. She couldn't think any more. She couldn't speak. She could only feel the sudden grip of terror freezing her muscles and her mind.

The man crossed in front of her. He was middle-aged, unshaven, and reeked of tobacco. Winnie tried to dodge him, but he stayed right at her elbow. When he reached for her again, Winnie froze.

She thought back to her famous primal scream, took a deep breath and planted her feet on the ground. But this time, not a sound came out of her mouth, as her eyes widened with fear . . .

*Coming this month: Book #1
in the exciting new series,
SPRING BREAK!*

*Join Alyssa, Gabrielle, and
Megan as they head to
Coconut Beach for the best
spring break ever!*

The red Mustang convertible sped down the highway, and a warm breeze tossed the girls' hair. Gabrielle glanced at Alyssa, who sat in the bucket seat next to her. "Are you okay?"

Alyssa smiled. Her eyes were still red from crying. "Much better, thanks."

Megan leaned forward. "Isn't fate weird?" she said. "Only a few days ago Gabby and I were each going to be spending spring break all alone in Leesville. Then I crash into her car, and Alyssa and Brock have a fight, and boom!" She popped her sunglasses down on her nose and giggled. "We're all spending our vacation together!"

"Well, it was a bit more complicated than that for me," Gabrielle pointed out.

Alyssa sighed. "And even more complicated for me. Only a few days ago my life was all planned out for me. Everyone thought I was going to marry Brock, go to the University of Georgia, and live happily ever after." She smiled bravely. "And up until a few months ago, even I thought that's exactly what I'd be doing. I never thought we'd end up *this* way . . ."

"Oh, come on," Megan said as she squeezed Alyssa's shoulder. "You and Brock will get back together. You'll get married, go to the University of Georgia, and live happily ever after, just like it was supposed to happen."

"I'm not so sure about that." Alyssa twisted the promise ring encircling her finger. "I'm not sure about anything anymore."

Gabrielle pushed her dark, windswept hair off her forehead. "We hardly know each other, Alyssa, so I don't mean to interfere. But I'd say go slowly. You're really young. You have plenty of time to get married."

"I've been trying to go slow," Alyssa replied. "But Brock, and his family, and my family, and even the kids at school keep pushing me toward the altar. My mother is the worst. She has dreams of throwing the biggest wedding celebration Leesville's ever seen."

"Hey, I think we're getting close," Gabrielle said excitedly. She took a deep breath. "You can smell the salt water in the air."

Alyssa closed her eyes and leaned back against her seat. "It's wonderful, isn't it? It makes me feel peaceful."

"Umm," Megan agreed distractedly. "It makes *me* think of sun, surf, and boys."

"*Everything* makes you think of boys," Gabrielle cracked.

Megan leaned over the front seat. "What's wrong with that?"

"Nothing," Gabrielle answered quickly. She wasn't about to ruin her good mood by arguing with Megan Becker about a topic as silly as boys.

"What about you, Alyssa?" Megan asked. "You must think a lot about boys."

"Well, not really. I mean, I think about Brock, of course." Alyssa tucked a strand of hair behind her ear and looked out at the low bushes bordering the highway. "Actually, I don't know all that much about boys."

"Ha!" Megan snorted. "That's a good one. You're the only one in this car who's ever had a steady boyfriend. You know more about boys than Gabby and me put together."

Alyssa turned to look at the other two girls. Even though her heart was torn by what had happened earlier with Brock, she actually felt good being with Gabrielle and Megan.

"Can I tell you both something?" Alyssa asked impulsively. "I want your solemn promise that what I'm going to tell you won't leave this car," she continued seriously.

"Promise," Gabrielle and Megan answered simultaneously.

"Brock is the only boy I've ever kissed. I've never even held hands with another boy."

Only the fact that Gabrielle was driving kept her from staring at Alyssa in amazement. Here was Leesville's Homecoming Queen, first runner-up for state Junior Miss, and the envy of every girl in Leesville, Georgia—and she had only kissed one boy.

"I never really had the opportunity," Alyssa continued. "I've been going out with Brock since we were freshmen."

Megan gave Alyssa's shoulder another squeeze. "It's time you started living. As soon as we get to Coconut Beach, we'll put on our bikinis . . ."

"I don't have a bikini," Alyssa cut in. "And anyway, I'm not so sure I'm ready to start 'living.' Nothing's settled with Brock."

"Yeah, Megan," Gabrielle added. "I think Alyssa needs some time to think before she joins you on a major boy hunt!"

"Well, all right. But when you're ready, Alyssa, and you too, Gabby, I'll be your personal guide to the boys of Coconut Beach."

Alyssa laughed nervously. "And to think I was on my way to Brock's grandmother's house."

"That was two hours ago, in a whole other lifetime." Megan leaned forward excitedly. "Trust me. This spring break is going to change our lives!"

As if to protest Megan's assertion, the Mustang suddenly sputtered and coughed.

"What's the matter?" Alyssa asked.

"I don't know." Gabrielle glanced at the dashboard. A red warning light was glowing on the instrument panel. "But I'll have to pull over."

Gabrielle steered the Mustang over to the shoulder of the highway just moments before it lurched to a dead stop.